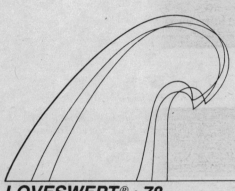

LOVESWEPT® • 78

Barbara Boswell
Sensuous Perception

BANTAM BOOKS
TORONTO • NEW YORK • LONDON • SYDNEY • AUCKLAND

SENSUOUS PERCEPTION

A Bantam Book / January 1985

ISBN 0-553-21688-0

Published simultaneously in the United States and Canada

Bantam Books are published by Bantam Books, Inc. Its
trademark, consisting of the words ''Bantam Books'' and the
portrayal of a rooster, is Registered in U.S. Patent and Trademark Office and in other countries. Marca Registrada. Bantam
Books, Inc., 666 Fifth Avenue, New York, New York 10103.

PRINTED IN THE UNITED STATES OF AMERICA

O   0 9 8 7 6 5 4 3 2 1

"I think I'm getting a telepathic message from you, Ashlee," Locke murmured huskily, lowering his lips to meet hers.

Ashlee yielded her mouth to him and clung to his strong frame, her eyes tightly shut as heated waves of sensual excitement washed over her. This was crazy, she thought dizzily. She and Locke were hopelessly incompatible, weren't they? Yet when he looked at her in that certain way, when he touched her, all her usually dependable common sense seemed to evaporate.

"This darned coat," Locke muttered some moments later, pulling her more tightly against him. "I'd like to tear it off you."

"Then I'd freeze." Ashlee managed a shaky little laugh. "Your Yankee winter weather is—"

"—too cold for a little Southern magnolia like you?" Locke teased, nipping at her neck with a dozen little playful kisses.

Ashlee tried to respond to the lightened mood, but she was aching for the satisfying pressure of his mouth on hers. "Locke," she whispered when she could stand it no more, "kiss me . . . kiss me hard."

Locke stared down into her soft brown eyes, then took her mouth with a ferocity that made her breath catch in her throat. Ashlee lost all sense of time and place as she gave herself up to the thrilling sensations erupting inside her. It was Locke, only Locke, who could make her feel this way . . .

WHAT ARE *LOVESWEPT* ROMANCES?

They are stories of true romance and touching emotion. We believe those two very important ingredients are constants in our highly sensual and very believable stories in the *LOVESWEPT* line. Our goal is to give you, the reader, stories of consistently high quality that may sometimes make you laugh, sometimes make you cry, but are always fresh and creative and contain many delightful surprises within their pages.

Most romance fans read an enormous number of books. Those they truly love, they keep. Others may be traded with friends and soon forgotten. We hope that each *LOVESWEPT* romance will be a treasure—a "keeper." We will always try to publish

LOVE STORIES YOU'LL NEVER FORGET
BY AUTHORS YOU'LL ALWAYS REMEMBER

The Editors

One

It was past five on a rainy Thursday in January and Ashlee Martin had already hung the Closed sign on the door of the small shop. Her partner had gone home early and Ashlee was counting the day's profits before leaving when the telephone began to ring.

It was her grandmother, calling from Shade Gap. Ashlee always knew when Gran was on the line. She picked up the receiver and said, "Hi, Gran," before her grandmother could speak a word.

Gran chuckled. "You've never been wrong yet," she said. Gran hadn't ever questioned Ashlee's uncanny "second sight," as she termed it. If something was missing, she asked Ashlee to locate it and Ashlee always did. No one could drop in unexpectedly on the Martin family; Ashlee always knew who was coming and when.

"Ashlee, a Detective Callahan called here for you. From Boston." Gran's voice rose in excitement. "I told him I wanted to give you the news myself."

Ashlee's heart began to pound. "He's found Amber."

"I wrote it all down for you, sugar," Gran said proudly. "Your twin sister was adopted from the Infants' Home in Philadelphia just three days after my Tommy and Carla got you. Her adoptive parents were from Massachusetts and their names are Bryce and Elizabeth Aames. Two A's in the Aames."

"Oh, Gran!" Ashlee's voice was barely a squeak. Her heart was pounding so hard, she could scarcely breathe. She leaned against the glass display counter, vaguely aware that tears were streaming down her cheeks. "W-what else?"

"Her name is still Amber Rose. They kept the name your birth mama gave her, just like Tommy and Carla kept yours."

"That's a good sign, isn't it, Gran?" Ashlee's mind was racing with excitement. "Our birth mother's middle name is Rose too. Caroline Rose Sheppard." Ashlee could visualize the original birth certificates she'd managed to get from the Department of Vital Statistics, thanks to a loophole in the Pennsylvania adoption law. "The name Rose is a connection among the three of us—Amber and me and our birth mother. Gran, maybe Amber and I could search for her together someday. We could write to—"

"Lord, child, fools rush in where angels fear to tread, but you rush in where fools fear to tread. You haven't even met your sister yet and you're already involving her in one of your wild plans."

"But I'm going to meet her, Gran! I'll leave tomorrow morning. I know Sandy will take over the shop and—"

"Ashlee!" Gran interrupted again. "Before you get packed and jump into your car, it would be a good idea to know where Amber is."

"Yes, ma'am," Ashlee agreed, and then she laughed, a shaft of pure happiness rushing through her. "Where is she?"

"She lives at Number One Aames Drive in a town

called Aames in Massachusetts." Gran paused and Ashlee knew she was frowning. "Oh, if only that Yankee agency in Philadelphia would have told my Tommy you had a twin. He and Carla would have been thrilled to take the both of you, and I could've raised you together, as the good Lord meant you to be. It's a sin to separate twin sisters," Gran added darkly. "Trust the Yankees to do it."

"But I've finally found my twin, Gran! And we're going to be together from now on!" Ashlee was too happy to bear a grudge toward anyone, even the Yankees who had kept her from her sister all these years. She'd known she had a twin even before she'd tracked down the original birth certificate that proved it. She'd felt her twin's presence—or absence—all her life, and not even the love of her foster grandmother and the rest of the multitudinous Martin clan could quite fill the void. She never questioned how she knew she had a sister, an identical twin sister, she just knew it.

"Psi ability" was the term used by the parapsychologists in Durham who had tested Ashlee over the years and found her highly gifted in the areas of clairvoyance and precognition. Yet her second sight hadn't enabled Ashlee to locate her twin. She'd had to hire a private detective to do that. George Callahan. And he had done it. He'd found her sister.

"Well, I know your heart is set on seeing your sister." Gran's voice interrupted Ashlee's reverie. "But be sure to call them up there and tell them you're coming. Amber Rose might not have the second sight and they might not appreciate a drop-in guest. I don't know a thing about Yankee hospitality, if there is such a thing, but they'd better treat my little girl right."

"Oh, they will, Gran, they will. Amber is going to be as thrilled as I am!"

"Steve Walton might not be so thrilled you're leaving, Ashlee."

"Oh." Ashlee grimaced. "Steve." She'd completely forgotten about him, yet another sign that he wasn't right for her. And lately those signs had been coming with disheartening frequency. "I guess I will have to call him and tell him I'm leaving."

"Darlin', you know we all wish you the best of luck with your sister. And give her our love. Your twin is one of us too, Ashlee."

Ashlee's eyes filled with grateful tears. "I love you, Gran." She began crying again. "And all the aunts and uncles and cousins too. Please don't believe that I love you all any less because I have to find my twin."

"Don't even think such nonsense," Gran admonished. "There is no limit on the love a heart can hold, Ashlee. Your twin sister is your own flesh and blood; she's a part of your heritage that's been missing all these years. You go to her, Ashlee."

Ashlee locked the cash in the small safe in the shop and drove to her apartment in an old frame house on a tree-lined street in Chapel Hill. The telephone number of Bryce Aames, Sr., was easily obtained from long distance directory assistance, and Ashlee dialed with trembling fingers. She'd already decided not to attempt to speak to Amber over the phone. Better to apprise her foster father of her own existence and let him give the good news to his daughter.

"Dad's out of town," a rather groggy voice said when the phone was picked up on the other end. "This is his son, Alec. May I take a message?"

Amber's brother! Ashlee couldn't keep her news to herself a moment longer. She told Alec who she was and eagerly recited the details of her long search for her sister. By the time Ashlee had finished her tale, Alec was almost as excited as she was. "You have to come up and meet Amber," he said enthusiastically. "We'll all want to meet you. As soon as possible."

"This weekend?" Ashlee suggested hopefully. She was already studying the road map spread out in front of her. The town of Aames was a dot on the map, above Boston and to the right of Cambridge.

"Sure, why not?" Alec boomed grandly. "Love to have you."

Sandy Marshall, Ashlee's partner and co-owner of Creativity, their doll and crafts boutique, agreed to run the shop alone during her absence. But as Gran had predicted, Steve Walton was less than thrilled about the trip to meet Amber.

Ashlee thought of his querulous reaction as she drove north along the interstate. They had been dating for several months now, and Steve had become increasingly demanding of her. Lately he'd begun to hint at marriage. The problem, Ashlee had come to realize, was that she didn't love him. Steve was a great date, but the better she came to know him, the more she recognized he should remain just that. A date. Not a husband. Ashlee's visions of marriage involved passion and love and an irrevocable commitment. She could foresee none of those things with Steve Walton. Sandy thought she was crazy. "Steve is a resident, soon to be a radiologist making big bucks," Sandy would continually say. "Why not force yourself to love the guy, Ash?" Maybe she was an unrealistic, starry-eyed romantic, Ashlee conceded, but Amber would understand. The thought comforted and elated her. She and Amber were twins, two of a kind. Amber would understand her.

Ashlee stayed overnight at a motel in New York. She wanted to get an early start the next morning and arrive at the Aameses' by lunchtime, but was exhausted from the drive and overslept. Then she worried about what to wear, admonishing herself at the same time for being nervous about the impression she wanted to make on her own sister. They were twins! The love between them was instinctual. She would wear what she liked and Amber would like it too.

Ashlee loved color, from the bold primary crayon colors to Easter-egg pastels. The only colors her wardrobe didn't contain were those she deemed non-colors: dreary black, somber navy, boring brown. Today she chose yellow jeans and a bright rainbow-striped sweater and pulled her dark honey-blond hair into a ponytail. Her hair had always been the bane of her existence. It was thick and poker straight, defying any attempts at curling. She had worn it short and she had worn it long. Once she'd even tried a perm, which hadn't taken, of course. Now the ponytail hung straight to the middle of her shoulder blades and Ashlee consoled herself with the thought that it was a practical style for driving. Anyway, Amber would have the same problem hair; in just a few hours they could bemoan it together.

She pulled on her well-worn boots and her pink, turquoise, and yellow ski jacket and loaded her bags into her little orange Rabbit. The backseat held three dolls, samples of her most popular designs. She'd brought them along for Amber. Ashlee loved making dolls and collected them too. She wondered if Amber shared this interest and hoped she did.

When she finally drove into the town of Aames in the middle of the afternoon, the car radio was blaring and Ashlee was singing along, giving her all to lyrics with a dramatic crescendo of a heart darkening into a total eclipse. She'd been singing for miles, her spirits soaring. However, she felt a flutter of uncertainty at the sight of a massive stone arch at the entrance of Aames Drive. The road was actually a long private driveway, the house visible nearly a half mile down. At least she thought it was a house. The immense stone and frame structure was bigger than the combined post office, sheriff's office, and jail, the largest building in Shade Gap. Did her sister actually live there?

Feeling nervous, Ashlee parked her car a few yards away from the house and walked to the front door. Given the imposing façade of the place, she half-expected to be greeted by a uniformed servant, and she rehearsed what she would say. She was tremendously relieved when a girl in her early teens opened the door after she'd rapped the large brass knocker several times.

"I'm Ashlee Martin and I'd like to see Amber Aames, please." Ashlee's voice was shaky, her cheeks flushed. She waited expectantly for the girl's welcoming cry of recognition. It never came.

"She's not here. She's at work, I think," the girl said flatly, eyeing Ashlee with bored disinterest.

"Not here?" Ashlee was acutely disappointed. Of course she and Sandy took turns working at the shop on Saturday, but it hadn't occurred to Ashlee that Amber wouldn't be waiting for her when she arrived.

"Wonder Woman works every day," the girl replied sullenly.

A sudden picture flashed before Ashlee's eyes of a large kitchen decorated in dull olive and yellow tones. There was a pot on the stove and hot liquid was bubbling over the sides. "Are you cooking something?" Ashlee asked, and the girl stared at her as if she'd taken leave of her senses. How to explain? "There's something boiling over on a stove," she began, not bothering to add that it might be in some other kitchen. She'd just happened to tune into the scene.

"My pudding!" the girl shrieked. "Oh, no!" She ran down the hall, leaving Ashlee standing on the doorstep, the door wide open. If she were sensible, as Sandy wished, if she weren't impulsive, as Steve accused, Ashlee would have gone back to her car and returned later to see Amber. But Ashlee being Ashlee, she entered the house and followed the sound of the young girl's shrieks. They led her to the kitchen where the girl, in a frantic attempt to remove the bubbling pot from the stove, had dropped it to the floor. A sticky, burned-smelling chocolate mess was everywhere, congealing on the stove and on the pristine linoleum floor. The girl was holding her reddened hand and crying.

"Did you burn your hand?" Ashlee dragged her to the sink and thrust her hand under a stream of cold water. "I'm sure it must hurt, but it doesn't look too bad."

"I wish I'd burned it off!" the girl cried. "Look at the mess! I'm going to get killed. I can't do anything right! I'm a stupid, clumsy misfit flop!"

Ashlee suppressed a smile. She'd almost forgotten how very dramatic adolescent girls could be. She'd rivaled Sarah Bernhardt at this child's age. "Of course you're not," she said kindly. "It was an accident. Everyone makes mistakes."

"Not in this house." The girl sniffled. "Oh, what am I going to do? Mrs. Bates, the cook, will be furious. She'll tell Daddy and everyone else and they'll all be angry."

"No one has to find out," Ashlee said soothingly, turning off the water. She dried the girl's hand carefully with a paper towel. "We'll clean it up right now."

"Are you kidding? This can never be cleaned up. They'll have to buy a new stove and put in a new floor and it will all have to come out of my allowance."

"You didn't see Aunt Judy's kitchen the time Jimmy Joe and Bubba decided to make brownies," Ashlee said. She removed her coat, rolled up her sleeves, and picked the charred pot up from the floor. "This is the minor leagues compared to that disaster, but we got it all cleaned up, as good as new. What's your name?" she asked as she searched under the sink for cleaning supplies.

"Sharon. Sharon Aames, Bryce, Jr.'s daughter." Sharon sank onto a chair. "I'm the untalented, uncoordinated, stupid one in the family."

"You're no such thing," Ashlee said as she began to scrub the stove. For the next half hour Sharon regaled her with a litany of the woes of being thirteen. Ashlee was on her hands and knees scrubbing the floor and listening to the tragedy of Sharon's C minus in general science when a deep masculine voice sounded in the hall.

"Mrs. Bates? Mrs. Bates!"

"Yikes!" Sharon leaped from her chair and disappeared into the pantry.

"Where's Mrs. Bates?"

Ashlee, still on her hands and knees, scrub brush in hand, found herself staring at a pair of men's loafers planted directly in front of her. She lifted her head slowly, her gaze traveling upward over a pair of Black Watch—plaid wool slacks and a dark green sweater to an unsmiling masculine face. A pair of gray-green eyes were staring down at her. Ashlee noted the man's thick dark hair parted carelessly to the side, the patrician nose, the strong jaw and chin so like Sharon's. He was about six feet two and Ashlee's neck was developing a crick from staring up so high.

"Where's Mrs. Bates?" the man asked again.

Ashlee decided to go for the obvious. "She's not here." The man scowled his displeasure and Ashlee saw the tiny lines around the corners of his eyes. She guessed his age to be somewhere in his thirties, maybe thirty-six or seven.

"Again? This is getting to be intolerable. Well, listen, when you get finished there, I'd like you to whip up a little snack for Cynthia and me. We'll be in the den." And then he was gone.

Sharon emerged from the pantry. Ashlee resumed scrubbing. "Who was that?" she asked.

"My uncle Locke. Locke Addison Aames, the future Nobel prizewinner. He does research at M.I.T. and teaches some graduate courses there in physics. He's written some books and won some awards in his field, I think it's thermodynamic physics. He's got his doctorate and has an IQ of about nine-hundred and ninety. Try telling *him* how you got a C minus in general science," Sharon added on an injured note.

"It wouldn't be easy." Ashlee hid a smile. Sharon's exaggerations tickled her. She replaced the cleaning supplies under the sink. "Who's this Cynthia I'm supposed to whip up a snack for? His wife?"

"Uncle Locke isn't married. My grandmother says he's never met a woman who's more interesting than physics to him. And he's so smart, most women bore him, Daddy says." Sharon's face darkened. "Cynthia is a snobbish, air-headed witch who wants to marry an Aames. She already tried to get my father, and when that didn't work, she decided to try Uncle Locke. I guess Uncle Alec will be next. He got divorced last year."

"Women bore him because he's so smart?" Ashlee was more interested in Locke than in Cynthia and her intentions toward the Aames men. "What about stupid men? Don't they bore him too?"

"Oh, Ashlee, men are smarter than women." Sharon sighed with a worldly wise air.

"I've never heard anything more ridiculous in my life!" Ashlee was appalled. "What do they teach you up here in these Yankee schools? Men smarter than women? Absurd! I have a whole passel of male cousins who shot that theory down in flames."

Sharon wasn't listening. She was admiring the spotless stove and floor. "Ashlee, you did it! It's perfect! I—I don't know how to thank you."

"I told you it wasn't anything that couldn't be set

right." Ashlee shrugged. "Now, what shall we whip up for your genius uncle and his friend?"

"You're not really going to do it, are you? You don't have to, Ashlee. I'll explain to Uncle Locke that you're—" Sharon broke off and stared at her in sudden consternation. "Who are you?"

Ashlee beamed. "Look closely at me, Sharon, and see if you can guess who I am."

Sharon stared, scrutinized, and finally shrugged. "You're not an Avon lady or something like that, are you?"

"I'm your aunt Amber's twin sister," Ashlee said, slightly exasperated. Maybe Sharon *was* a little thick. "Her identical twin. We were separated at birth and adopted by different families and I've finally found her after years of searching."

"Aunt Amber's twin?" Sharon shrieked. "Seriously? Honestly?"

"Don't I look like her?" Perhaps she and Amber weren't identical twins after all. "Not even a little?"

"Well, you do have the same eyes." Sharon studied Ashlee's face intently. "A pretty chocolate brown. And your nose is like hers, and your mouth. But your hair is different. Yeah, I guess you do sort of look like her but—wow! Are you two different! It's awesome!"

"For sure," Ashlee countered dryly. Sharon's assessment was a little too hazy to be relied upon. "I'll fix that snack now." She needed to do something to pass the time. "What do you think they'd like?"

"Something gross, like raw cauliflower." Sharon made a face. "Uncle Locke is heavily into health and Cynthia pretends to be."

Ashlee opened the refrigerator and inspected the contents of the vegetable drawer. There was a supply of carrots, radishes, cauliflower, and celery. Though not physically related to the Martins, she had acquired their eating tastes, and raw radishes for a snack held no appeal. A snack was something sweet and satisfying and delicious. "I've got it," she said, spying a bunch of bananas in a hanging basket. "Get me three eggs, Sharon."

Ten minutes later the batch of deep-fried banana fritters were done, and Ashlee dusted them with powdered sugar and arranged them on a plate.

"Hey, these are good!" Sharon munched one as she led the way from the kitchen to the den. "Kind of like fried pies, which we aren't supposed to eat. Grandmother says junk food rots your teeth and brain.

"That conjures up a pleasant image," Ashlee murmured, remembering how she and her cousins used to pour chocolate milk over their Froot Loops. But none of them had ever had a single cavity. She followed Sharon through the hall, this time taking note of her surroundings. The place was filled with Oriental rugs, eighteenth-century antique English furniture, polished silver, and seascapes—exactly the way she would expect a conservative, wealthy Yankee home to be. Probably the house had looked the same a hundred years ago and would still be the same a hundred years hence.

"There's the den," Sharon whispered, but did not enter the room. Ashlee did, carrying the plate of banana fritters and some paper towels. Fritters tended to leave the fingers very greasy.

"Here's your snack, sir." Ashlee smiled at Locke Aames as she set the platter on the table in front of the sofa. Cynthia was sitting close to Locke, her shoes off and her feet tucked under her. The skirt of her neat little burgundy wool dress was casually but seductively arranged just above her knees. She was an attractive brunette with short, wavy hair and wide-set blue eyes. Locke's arm was around her, resting just below the underside of her breast.

Neither Locke nor Cynthia glanced at Ashlee. Both were staring at the banana fritters piled on the plate. "Are those . . . fried?" Cynthia recoiled in horror, as if a poisonous snake were curled beneath the fritters.

"Southern deep-fried banana fritters," amended Ashlee.

"How . . . interesting." Cynthia laid her hand on Locke's arm, her burgundy nail polish a startling contrast to the dark green of his sweater. "But I think I'll pass. I'm not really hungry."

"Same here," Locke said. "You can take them away now."

"You're not going to eat anything?" Ashlee's face clouded. Her brows drew together and her jaw clenched. The Martins would have known to take cover, but Locke and Cynthia remained placidly on the sofa. Ashlee's tone became more militant. "You said you wanted a snack and I fixed you something special and now you're not even going to *try* it?"

Locke looked up to meet her outraged glare. "How long did you say you'll be replacing Mrs. Bates?" he asked pointedly. And then his jaw dropped. He sat up straight and stared at her, his eyes widening.

But Ashlee was fuming too much to notice. She folded her arms across her chest and continued to glower. "I didn't say. Now, are you going to eat a banana fritter—or not?"

No one was more surprised than Locke Aames himself when he reached for a fritter and bit into it. He swallowed hard. "Not bad," he murmured politely, placing it back on the plate. He gave Ashlee another long, puzzled stare and then shook his head, as if to banish his confusion.

"If it's not bad, why don't you finish it?" Ashlee demanded.

"It's not bad if you have a taste for the sweet, the fried, and the greasy, which it happens, I do not," Locke retorted.

Cynthia giggled. Ashlee was not amused. He hated her delicious fritters; she should have just given him a head of raw cauliflower. She picked up the offending platter and was halfway to the door when Sharon burst in, accompanied by a younger boy of about ten.

"This is my brother Brian, Ashlee," Sharon said while grabbing fritters with both hands. Brian followed her lead and Ashlee smiled fondly at them. They reminded her of the younger Martin cousins.

"Children, I'm entertaining a guest," Locke said dampeningly, rising to his feet. "I would appreciate it if you went elsewhere. And please don't stuff yourselves with those—those . . ." He paused, searching for the appropriate word.

"Those what?" Ashlee threw him her most threatening glare.

"Er—banana fritters." Locke stared at her, clearly nonplussed by her defiant attitude.

"Ashlee's a guest too," Sharon said in a tone of voice that would have earned her a swat in the Martin family. "You thought she was a maid, but she's not. She's Aunt Amber's twin sister and she's come all the way from North Carolina to see her."

"What?" Cynthia was on her feet now too.

"What are you talking about, Sharon?" Locke asked.

"Aunt Amber and Ashlee are twin sisters who were adopted by different families," explained Brian, who had obviously been filled in on the facts by his sister.

"Ashlee's spent years trying to find her sister and she finally found her and came here to see her and you thought she was the maid." Sharon snickered. "What an awful way to treat such a special guest! Boy, are you rude, Uncle Locke!"

A dark red flush stained Locke's neck and spread slowly to his face. Apparently Sharon's remarks had hit their target. He gazed at Ashlee in dawning wonder. "I thought you looked . . ." His eyes narrowed and his face became shuttered. Ashlee could almost see the conflict raging within him: whether to believe his eyes or demand irrefutable proof. The rational scientist within him won. "I take it you do have documented evidence of your claim?"

What a stiff, Ashlee thought with rising irritation. His brother, Alec, had accepted her word over the phone, sight unseen. Alec . . . She frowned. She'd told him she was coming; he'd actually invited her. Then why was her presence such a surprise to Locke? Ashlee's frown deepened. Sharon hadn't known anything about her either, although at the time she'd put that down to a child's ability to forget anything that didn't pertain directly to herself. "I called Thursday morning and spoke to Alec Aames," Ashlee said. "He invited me to come up this weekend. Didn't he mention it?"

"Uncle Alec was in bed all day Thursday," Brian piped up. "He was sick, wasn't he, Uncle Locke?"

"Er—yes." Locke nodded.

"He was hung over," Sharon said, chortling. "I met him coming in from a party on my way out to the school bus that morning. He said he felt like a herd of buffalo was stampeding inside his head."

"I can see why he forgot to mention that I called," Ashlee said dryly. So Amber didn't even know she was coming today? Ashlee's face lit up in a smile. *That* was why Amber hadn't been here to meet her. She glanced at Locke, who was studying her intently from across the room.

"I do have the documented evidence you requested," Ashlee told him coolly. "I have both Amber's and my own original birth certificates and adoption papers from the Philadelphia court."

Locke crossed the room in three giant strides, caught her by the arm, and hauled her over to the window. In the glare of the afternoon winter sun he examined her face feature by feature, holding her chin with one hand, her shoulder with the other. "It's an incredible story," he said, tilting her chin, analyzing her from that particular angle with the thoroughness of a scientist inspecting a laboratory animal for test results. "A stupid plot right out of

Dickens," he continued to mutter to himself as he turned her head to another angle. "But the eyes, the nose, the mouth. God, even the shape of the ears . . ."

Ashlee was debating whether or not to endure the inspection with a modicum of dignity or to kick his shins and brain him with the banana fritters, when her eyes happened to collide with his.

I'm going to marry him. The thought flashed through her mind as she gazed into the gray-green depths of his eyes. There was no accompanying emotion or fluttering pulses, simply a definite, certain knowledge. This was the man she was going to marry.

Immediately Ashlee sought to refute the notion. She was wrong; she had to be. Marry Locke Aames, her twin's foster brother? A man whose chosen profession, thermo-something physics, she could barely pronounce? She didn't even know what it was! Marry a stiff, stuffy Yankee who cozied up on the couch with Cynthia and rejected her banana fritters? Who mistook her for the maid?

Ashlee jerked away from him. She'd been wrong before, hadn't she? Not all her perceptions were correct; she wasn't infallible. Hadn't she been positive that she and Amber were identical twins? She'd obviously been wrong there. Marry Locke Aames? She didn't even like the man! And he certainly didn't like her. No, it was preposterous. Perhaps Sharon's formidable grandmother was right and all the junk food she had consumed over the years was taking its toll on her brain.

"I'd like to see the birth certificates and adoption papers, if I may." Locke's face was rather pale, his voice unsteady.

"Of course. They're in my purse." Ashlee's voice was unsteady too. She was shaking. She just couldn't seem to chase the crazy thought away. She might protest it or rationalize or rail against fate, but she couldn't shake the deadly certain knowledge. Locke Aames was the man she was going to marry.

"Your purse is in the kitchen, Ashlee. I'll get it," Sharon volunteered. Brian continued to help himself to the banana fritters.

"Amber is certainly going to be surprised," Cynthia said, smirking slightly. "What part of North Carolina are you from?"

Not, Ashlee could tell, that Cynthia felt *any* part was worth being from. "From Shade Gap, ma'am," Ashlee drawled, allowing her accent to become thick and pronounced. "It's a li'l ole village deep in the Great Smoky Mountains."

Sharon returned with her purse, and Ashlee removed the documents and handed them to Locke. Her fingers brushed his as he took the papers and she drew back as if burned. Marry this man? There was clairvoyance and there was absurdity and this outlandish perception was clearly a case of the latter. She watched Locke peruse the original birth certificates and the adoption papers. She was going to marry Locke Aames.

Ashlee swallowed. Extra-sensory perception was in general the acquisition of knowledge through other than sensory means. And ESP took two forms. Clairvoyance was extra-sensory perception pertaining to external objects or events; precognition was the same, only in the future. In the many tests given her, she'd scored exceptionally high in both areas.

But that didn't mean she was a fortune-teller, Ashlee argued with herself. Dr. Cameron would shudder at the notion. What was thoroughly disconcerting was that she'd never had such an intuitive feeling concerning her future with any other man. Not even with Steve Walton, not even when she was kissing a man. She tried to picture herself kissing Locke Aames and shuddered. He wasn't her type, not at all. He was too tall, too thin, too dark, too Yankee, too stiff, too brainy, too everything! And who wanted to marry an award-winning physicist with an insufferably high IQ, a health-crazed esthete who lived on raw vegetables? She liked to laugh and have fun; she wanted passion and shared companionship. Locke Aames was the antithesis of all her dreams. Who ever heard of a fun-loving thermodynamic physicist? It was a contradiction in terms. Cynthia was welcome to him!

Locke handed her back the papers. "I didn't really need to see them to believe you," he said quietly. "As soon as I noticed the resemblance, I knew you had to be Amber's twin. It was such a shock, you see. I . . . usually don't even think of Amber as being adopted. Having her twin appear out of nowhere really threw me."

Ashlee tucked the papers into her purse. "You think that we, Amber and I, resemble each other?" He had a nice voice when he wasn't barking out orders, she caught herself thinking. Deep, masculine, resonant.

"Putting aside the differences in weight and hairstyle," Locke said, "it's obvious that the two of you are identical twins."

Two

Ashlee's lungs seemed to constrict, and for a moment she couldn't breathe.

"I'm terrible sorry I mistook you for the maid." Locke's face again reddened slightly at the memory. "You have to understand that the housekeeping situation around here sometimes borders on the farcical. Mrs. Bates, the cook, regularly goes off on benders and Anna, the housekeeper, has to call an agency for temporary replacements. Three days ago Anna's husband, who is also our grounds-keeper and gardener, was hospitalized for an ulcer, so Anna hasn't been around either. My parents are in Florida for the winter and—" He smiled ruefully. "I'm babbling. I feel like a complete fool for thinking you were a servant."

"Everyone makes mistakes," Ashlee said quickly. He really did seem upset, although she wasn't sure if it was remorse for treating her like a servant or embarrassment for making a faux pas. She had the impression that Locke Aames was a man of few mistakes. "There was no harm done."

He stared at her. "But, if you don't mind my asking, why were you scrubbing the kitchen floor?"

Ashlee caught Sharon's eye and read the heartfelt plea. "I'm hyperactive," she improvised. "I had to do something while I was waiting for Amber so I—uh—scrubbed the floor." Remembering the chocolate mess, she couldn't help but add, "It really needed to be done."

Sharon giggled. Brian finished the last banana fritter and burped.

"Now I know how Alice felt when she fell into the rabbit hole," Cynthia complained. "Locke, couldn't she wait with the children in some other room while we resume our conversation?"

Conversation, ha! Ashlee glanced from Cynthia to Locke. They'd been on the verge of a necking session; that had been plain enough to see. "I'll be happy to wait somewhere else with Sharon and Brian"—she looked at Locke mockingly—"so you and Cynthia can resume your . . . conversation."

"No! No, of course you won't be exiled with the children." Locke caught her arm when she would have walked away. "We haven't even been properly introduced. I from know your papers that you're Ashlee Martin. I'm Locke Aames." He turned to include the sulky Cynthia in the introduction. "And this is Cynthia Lowell, a family friend. So, Ashlee, you're from the—er—mountains?"

Obviously less than pleased at having been relegated to the nebulous position of family friend, Cynthia barely managed a stiff little nod. "A real down-home girl. How quaint."

"Well, I'm right pleased to meetcha, folks." Ashlee lapsed again into heavy Shade Gap-ese. What a shame she wasn't chewing bubble gum. A large popping bubble would have fit right in with the character they had attributed to her.

"You're a great cook, Ashlee," Brian said. "Will you make me some more banana fritters?"

"Sure I will, sugar. And maybe I can whip up

some hush puppies and hog jowls since your cook isn't here. Those are two of our biggest sellers at the diner," she added confidentially.

"You work in a diner?" Locke asked a bit too heartily.

"When they don't need me to pump gas." It was only a partial untruth, Ashlee decided. The Martin clan did own the Shade Gap Diner and adjoining filling station, and while growing up she and all the other cousins had taken turns working in both. No need to mention her apartment in Chapel Hill or Creativity's success. These Yankee snobs wanted to see her as a hillbilly yokel, and she would give them what they so richly deserved.

"You work in a gas station too?" Brian sounded envious.

"Yep. It's a combo gas station and diner, the most popular truck stop in Shade Gap. Also the only one."

"We're going to have to call the paramedics to revive poor Amber when she meets her twin," Cynthia said under her breath to Locke. Ashlee wasn't supposed to have heard, but she did, every word.

And Locke knew it. He looked terribly embarrassed and moved away from Cynthia. "I assume you plan to stay and visit with Amber for a while, Ashlee. I'd like to invite you to stay here at the house. In fact, I insist on it. Sharon can show you to one of the guest rooms."

"The blue one on the third floor?" asked Sharon.

"No, the yellow one with the adjoining bath on the second. I've always thought that was the best bedroom in the house."

He was trying to make up for Cynthia's nastiness and, perhaps, his own earlier rudeness, but Ashlee felt an inexplicable wave of hostility toward him. She didn't want Locke Aames to be nice to her. For reasons she didn't care to analyze, she preferred his rudeness and condescension.

"I hear a car!" Sharon exclaimed. She rushed to

the window and peered out. Ashlee stood on tiptoe behind her and caught a glimpse of dark green flash by the window. "Is it Amber?" Her voice was taut with anticipation.

"It's only Uncle Alec," Sharon said, groaning.

"We were hoping you were Aunt Amber," Brian announced to the tall dark man in navy and white running clothes who bounded into the room a minute later.

"Sorry to disappoint you, kid." Uncle Alec ruffled Brian's hair. "Do I have time to shower before dinner? I did ten miles today and I'm afraid I'm a little rank."

"Take all the time you need, Alec. There isn't going to be any dinner," Locke said. "Mrs. Bates is nowhere to be found and Anna isn't around either. It's take-out city tonight."

"Unless Ashlee cooks up a batch of hog jowls and corn pone," Cynthia said sweetly.

"I wouldn't dream of asking our guest to work," Locke interjected quickly. He cast Ashlee what she knew was meant to be a supportive glance. She didn't need the support; a twit like Cynthia didn't bother her, but the fact that he seemed to think she did was rather telling. Didn't Cynthia realize that she was scoring no points by demeaning Ashlee? The woman was literally forcing Locke over to Ashlee's side.

"Alec, Amber has a surprise awaiting her," Cynthia went on, her blue eyes glittering. Locke cleared his throat and edged closer to Ashlee.

"Meet Amber's long-lost twin from the Smoky Mountains in North Carolina. Ashlee Martin, a gas station attendant and waitress in a truck stop." Cynthia's voice rose gleefully.

Ashlee shook her head. Poor Cynthia. That was definitely a negative volley. Had the woman no perception at all? Locke was clearly disapproving. He glared at Cynthia and draped a protective arm around Ashlee's shoulders. Ashlee's first impulse was to shrug it off, but when she saw the expression on Cynthia's face, she was seized by what Gran called a "devil imp." She allowed herself to lean into Locke's hard, lean body and smiled up at him, her most winning smile, the smile that showed the dimple in her left cheek, so angelic and adorable a smile that when she'd used it on the Martins, Gran invariably asked, "What kind of trouble did you get yourself into this time, miss?"

Locke drew a sudden sharp breath and stared into her brown eyes. She gazed up at him, wondering if her special, heart-melting smile, usually saved to extricate herself from disasters, would be overdoing it a tad.

"Ashlee, of course!" Alec knocked his forehead with his hand. "We talked on Thursday. Oh, no!" This time he heaved a dramatic groan. "I forgot to tell Amber, actually I forgot to tell anyone. You see, I wasn't feeling—um—quite myself on Thursday. I'd spent the day in bed and after you called, I fell back to sleep and . . ." He continued to rattle on and Ashlee studied him with interest. Alec was younger than Locke and was a breathtakingly handsome man, his features classically perfect, his physique male-centerfold material. As Ashlee looked at him, no perceptions flashed to mind. She thought he was incredibly good-looking and guessed that women must throw themselves at his feet, but not once was she seized by the insane notion that she would marry him. She glanced at Locke.

While there was a family resemblance between the brothers, Locke's features were too sharp, too compellingly masculine to place him in the Greek-god category with Alec. And though Locke's body was hard and lean, he lacked the carefully sculpted muscles that flexed beneath Alec's form-fitting sweat suit. Glancing from brother to brother, Ashlee's heart abruptly sank. It was no longer a cognitive flash. The knowledge had settled into her consciousness and been absorbed. She was going to marry Locke Aames. Only the fact that he didn't know it yet saved her from total misery.

"This is absolutely amazing, Ashlee. I'm so delighted to meet you." Alec took her hand in his. "Imagine! Our Amber having a twin sister. I feel as if we've been doubly blessed." Alec's smile was so sincere, so melting, that Ashlee knew he practiced it in front of a mirror. She ought to recognize the signs; she used to rehearse her own smiles all through high school. She had a smile for any occasion. Once her cousin Willie had caught her practicing her sexy smile and he'd teased her so unmercifully that she'd stopped smiling altogether for a week.

Locke Aames never practiced his smiles, of that Ashlee was certain. He probably glanced into the mirror once a day to shave and carelessly comb his hair, and that would be that.

"Thank you, Alec," she drawled, right in character, batting her lashes and treating him to her own version of the melting smile. "It's a real pleasure to meet you too. Y'all have been so sweet to me, I feel like I'm family already."

Ashlee realized that Locke still had his arm around her when his fingers gripped her shoulder tightly. Too tightly. She looked up to find him staring at her grimly. And Cynthia was positively breathing fire.

"Ashlee is going to have the yellow room on the second floor, Uncle Alec," Sharon said. "But I wish she was going to be on the third floor with me."

"I like the idea of your being on the second floor, Ashlee." Alec's smile topped her own in the charm category. He was flirting with her, Ashlee realized with some amusement. She guessed Alec Aames was the type to flirt with any female; he exuded that certain practiced appeal. "You'll be in our wing. We'll be neighbors."

"And I've always been the neighborly type." Ashlee winked.

Locke hissed under his breath. He didn't approve, Ashlee thought gleefully. Did he actually believe her stupid enough to fall for Alec's all too obvious game? "Does the whole Aames family live in this house?" she asked, smiling at both brothers.

"Yes," they answered in unison. "This is home to all of us," Alec continued. "Mother, Father, Locke, Amber, me, our older brother, Bryce, Sharon and Brian's father, and, of course, Sharon and Brian." He winked at his niece and nephew.

"Just like the Carringtons on *Dynasty*," Ashlee said. "All those people under the same roof."

"We wouldn't know," Sharon said, pouting. "We're not allowed to have television in this house. It's another Aames family rule."

"No TV?" Ashlee was incredulous. "None at all?"

"We believe in utilizing our leisure time more constructively," Locke explained with a kindly, patient air that set Ashlee's teeth on edge. "There are so many interesting alternatives to passively sitting in front of a television set. Reading or studying or playing a musical instrument or listening to good music."

"And I take it your idea of good music isn't Michael Jackson or Men At Work?" Ashlee asked dryly. She tried to imagine growing up without television and failed utterly. Gran and her aunts and uncles adored TV; they were always discussing their favorite shows. The Martin children had followed suit. To this day Ashlee and her family discussed episodes of their favorite programs, long distance!

"Michael Jackson!" Sharon flopped into a chair in a mock swoon. "I absolutely adore him!"

"And we watch TV too," Brian added defiantly. "At our friends' houses. We watch everything—cartoons and reruns and R-rated movies on cable."

"You seemed surprised that the Aames family lives together in this house," Cynthia said, deftly steering the conversation around to Ashlee again, her voice artificially sweet. "Don't all you mountain folks live together? Twenty to a room or something?"

"There were about a dozen of us in the cabin," Ashlee replied ingenuously. "Uncle Billy and his family would sleep in a '48 Buick in the front yard. Uncle Bo and his kids had a lean-to in the back."

Alec, Sharon, and Brian believed her. So did Cynthia. Locke's eyes narrowed thoughtfully. "I think you're stringing us along, Ashlee," he surprised her by saying. "And maybe deservedly so. Am I correct?"

"Well, it's true the whole Martin clan lives close by on Martin land, but my grandmother and each of her five sons, my uncles and their families, have their own houses," Ashlee confessed. "Complete with electricity and indoor plumbing."

"So." Locke looked down on her and his gray-green eyes held something, some indefinable challenge, that made her nerve endings tingle oddly. "You're a bit of a tease, are you?"

Ashlee carefully removed his hand from her shoulder and gave him a cool little smile. "So I've been told."

It didn't require telepathy to know that at that moment, for the first time, Locke was sexually aware of her. His gaze traveled over the fullness of her breasts, braless beneath the rainbow-striped sweater, the soft flare of her hips and shapely jean-clad legs, then returned to her face. He was staring at her mouth, seemingly fascinated by the sensual curve of her lower lip, and Ashlee decided to raise the physicist's own personal thermodynamics. She parted her lips softly, and provocatively ran the tip of her tongue along the inner rim of her mouth. Locke swallowed visibly.

"A white Mercedes is turning onto the road from

the intersection." The scene flashed vividly through Ashlee's mind and she knew at once who the driver must be. "It's Amber's car, isn't it?"

Sharon and Brian raced to the window. "I don't see any car," Brian said.

"That's because she said it was at the intersection. You can't see the intersection from here," Sharon informed him scornfully.

"Then how—" Brian began, but was abruptly interrupted by his Uncle Alec. "Amber does have a white Mercedes, it was her twenty-first-birthday gift from the folks. But how did you know that, Ashlee?"

"She's turning into the drive," Brian announced, his voice high with excitement. "Aunt Amber is home!"

Ashlee couldn't remain still a moment longer. Her heart racing and her whole body trembling, she ran from the room and through the hall to the large front entrance foyer. Sharon and Brian were right behind her and, following at a more decorous pace, were Locke, Alec, and Cynthia. This wasn't the way Ashlee had envisioned the reunion with her sister, in the austere Aames foyer surrounded by strangers, but she'd learned that reality often didn't match one's fantasy. What was important did hold true: she was going to be with her twin sister at last.

At five forty-eight on Saturday, January twentieth, Ashlee Rose Martin and Amber Rose Aames came face-to-face after a separation of twenty-four years, nine months, and three weeks. Ashlee was grateful that Brian greeted Amber first, confirming her identity, for even though blessed with psi ability, Ashlee would have never recognized her twin as her own. The gaunt young woman in the hall was clutching a formidably sized executive briefcase and was dressed for success in what must surely be by now a uniform—a severely tailored dark blue suit, a white man-tailored shirt, and depressingly sensible low-heeled shoes. And if Amber shared Ashlee's periodic disgust with her hair, she had taken drastic measures to combat the problem. Amber's hair was so short that for a terrible moment Ashlee wondered if her sister had undergone brain surgery and had her head shaved; the resultant half-inch length covering her head could be new growth. But if that were the case, surely one of the Aameses would have mentioned it beforehand. It seemed logical to assume that this was her sister's chosen hair style and it did fit right in with the stark suit, shirt, and shoes. Amber wore no makeup or jewelry save a man-sized watch with a one-inch leather band.

And she was so thin! Ashlee wasn't overweight at all, but she outweighed Amber by perhaps ten to fifteen pounds. Where Ashlee's figure was feminine and curved, Amber's was straight and androgynous. Her sister had no breasts or hips, Ashlee noted with shock. Her cheeks were sunken and her legs were like two sticks. The weight difference belied the similarity of their features as well. The eyes were the same color and shape, but Amber's seemed hollow, her nose appeared sharper. Ashlee couldn't tear her eyes away from that too thin face. Maybe Amber had been sick!

Her eyes wide with compassion and alarm, Ashlee introduced herself. How many hours had she spent daydreaming about this moment? And in every single dream both twins had been thrilled to find each other. They would embrace eagerly, laughing and weeping, the years and long separation erased by their instinctive mutual kinship.

"My twin sister?" Amber repeated flatly, staring at Ashlee as if she were an extra-terrestrial who'd dropped in from some undiscovered galaxy. She looked beyond Ashlee to Locke and Alec. "All right, guys, let me in on the joke."

"It's not a joke, Amber. She has the papers to prove it," Locke said soberly. "Original birth certificates, adoption papers. It all computes, Amber. This is your twin."

Everyone was staring at them. Ashlee wanted to drag her sister into another room, away from the crowd of curious onlookers, and throw her arms around her, to tell her how much she'd missed her over the years, how long and hard she'd searched for her. She stared into Amber's brown eyes, so like her own, and experienced the thrill of at last looking at someone related to her by blood. She and Amber shared the same parents; they had even shared the same womb. There was so much that she wanted to say to her twin, but Amber was staring at her so strangely, her expression changing from one of blank disbelief to incredulity and finally—Ashlee hoped she was wrong—to anger?

"We—we have so much to talk about," Ashlee began tentatively, aware of the vibrations emanating from Amber and refusing to believe it could be hostility. "I want to know everything about you."

"I drew up a biographical sketch when I applied to Harvard Business School," Amber replied coolly, her gaze fastened on the brilliant stripes of Ashlee's sweater. She shuddered. "I believe I have a duplicate copy if you care to read it."

"Amber." Locke's voice held a warning note that Amber responded to immediately.

"I'm a graduate of Radcliffe and I'm currently working on my MBA at Harvard while I hold a junior executive position at the family bank in Boston. Aames Bank, perhaps you've heard of it?" Amber paused long enough for Ashlee to shake her head no. "It has branches throughout the Boston area and was founded by my great-grandfather, Carleton Addison Aames. *His* great-grandfather founded this town, Aames, and the family has lived here ever since. The Aames family has been in this country since the middle of the seventeenth century when John James Aames emigrated from

England and became one of the original proprietors of the Province of New Jersey. He was a signer of the Colonial Charter 'Concessions and Agreements' in 1676," she ended proudly.

"Amber, I don't think Ashlee is interested in the history of the Aames family," Alec said, smiling tenderly. "She wants to know about you personally."

Amber paled. "I'm an Aames." Her voice shook. "It's the most important part of my identity. Are you telling me not to discuss the Aames family history because I'm not really an Aames?"

"Of course you're an Aames," Locke interjected warmly.

Ashlee stared from one to another. What was going on here? Amber seemed as obsessed with the Aames family as Ashlee herself had been in finding her twin and learning more of her biological heritage.

"Ashlee wants to know your interests and hobbies, Amber," Locke added, watching both twins. "Shall I tell her how well you play the flute? And that your favorite composer is Debussy?" There was a brief silence. "Amber loves to read too," Locke persisted with determined cheerfulness. "Particularly history. I believe you've just finished Will and Ariel Durant's ten-volume set of *The Story of Civilization*, haven't you, Amber?"

"Eleven," Amber corrected him. "There are eleven volumes."

"Oh." Ashlee stared at her. For the first time in her life she was at a loss for words. History had been her worst subject in school, and she'd assiduously avoided it since graduation. She'd never heard of Debussy and wasn't particularly enamored of flute music, not that she'd ever heard much of it. "Eleven volumes," she repeated. And her sister had read them all?

"Aren't you going to tell Amber about yourself, Ashlee?" Cynthia said sweetly. "Life in the Great

Smokies, the gas station, your favorite television programs?"

Ashlee watched Amber's face as her sister's eyes flicked over her tousled ponytail, her bright clothes, and scuffed boots. *She doesn't like me.* The thought left Ashlee thunderstruck. Amber was not glad she'd been found, was not thrilled to discover she had a twin, and was not going to love her sister instinctively and unconditionally.

"I don't think I'm up to coping with this at this point in time," Amber said in her brisk, strident voice. "I've had a long day. At the bank in the morning, in class all afternoon. I'm going upstairs to shower and change. I have a date at seven."

Everyone watched in silence as Amber swiftly climbed the wide staircase, her briefcase swinging at her side. Ashlee stared at the faded Oriental figures in the well-worn rug on the floor. She wasn't going to cry, she promised herself, and she wasn't giving up. She'd known for years that she had a twin; Amber hadn't known until a few minutes ago. And to be confronted with the knowledge and the person at the same time, after a long, hard day . . . Of course Amber had been upset and unsure.

Ashlee felt her spirits rise a little. She had always been an optimist. *Ashlee is always looking for the silver lining,* Gran often said. And she was stubborn too. No, she wasn't giving up in defeat after a less than promising start. She and Amber *would* be friends. It was just going to take some time, that's all.

"I didn't want to tell you that Aunt Amber is a total space cadet," Sharon said, her voice rousing Ashlee from her reverie. She wasn't sure what a total space cadet was, but from Sharon's tone it was not a complimentary term. "I was hoping she'd change the minute she saw you, like in the movies. I guess I should have warned you, Ashlee."

Ashlee managed a smile. "Amber is a little different from what I expected but . . . I love her already.

I know we're going to be close friends." She happened to glance in Locke's direction. He was staring at her in such a strange way. Their eyes met and clung for several long moments, and Ashlee felt her cheeks begin to grow warm. She averted her eyes, but she could still feel him watching her.

"Why don't we bring your things in from the car, Ashlee," Locke said, crossing the hall to stand beside her. "You can get settled in your room and then we'll think about where to go for dinner."

Ashlee nodded and followed him outside, grateful for the reprieve from the others' speculation. It was cold and she shivered, her breath visible in the early darkness of the evening.

"You should have worn a coat." The cold temperatures didn't appear to bother Locke. "Where is it, in the kitchen?" He put his arm around her and drew her against his side. "Do you want to go back inside for it?"

"No." Ashlee kept walking, but stayed close to the warmth of his body. "I'm okay."

"Ashlee, there is something that is puzzling me. When you saw Amber's car at the intersection . . ." Locke frowned and Ashlee tensed, guessing what he would say next. "The intersection isn't visible from the house."

This was hardly the time or place to delve into the subject of clairvoyance. "Did I say intersection? Goodness, I meant to say I saw it coming up the drive." Ashlee hoped she sounded sufficiently confused. "I've been in such a tizzy all day, waiting for Amber. I thought she was expecting me, too, you see, and I had visions of one of those out-of-the-movies reunion scenes." She lapsed into silence, remembering the expression on her sister's face. "I guess it was a scene from a horror movie from Amber's point of view."

"Ashlee, I feel I ought to apologize for Amber," Locke began uncertainly. "You see, she takes being an Aames very seriously. She always has. Bryce,

Alec, and I have never really taken the family genealogy all that seriously, but Amber lives and breathes it. She has some complex about excelling because the Aameses always have. She went to Radcliffe because it was Mother and Grandmother's alma mater and spent every waking minute studying, absolutely determined to graduate summa cum laude like me, or magna cum laude like Bryce and Alec. As it was she nearly wrecked her health. She developed mononucleosis and bleeding ulcers and had to be hospitalized several times. She did graduate with honors in spite of all her health problems, but she was crushed because she didn't feel that it was high enough."

"She graduated from a school like Radcliffe with honors and she didn't feel she'd done well?" Ashlee was awed. "Why, Gran and the Martins thought that my cousins and I were marvels because we decided to stay in high school. We were the first generation of high school graduates in the family," she added with a touch of pride.

"Amber has always been her own worst critic," Locke explained. "The family never set such exalted standards for her; it was all Amber's doing."

"You and Bryce and Alec aren't adopted, are you?"

"No. Our parents wanted a daughter and finally had one the year my brothers and I were nine, eleven, and thirteen. I remember it very well. The baby was premature and died before she was a week old. Mother was devastated. A family friend told us about the Infants' Home in Philadelphia. Babies were in plentiful supply there in those days. Six months later they adopted Amber. We were never told that she was a twin," he added almost apologetically.

Poor Amber, a replacement baby. Ashlee's heart went out to her twin. And Amber felt obligated to be that full-blooded Aames daughter who had died in infancy. Whether self-imposed or not, it was a difficult burden to bear. How much easier life had been with the accepting, warm, easy-to-please Martins.

"Amber wanted to join our father, Bryce, and Alec at the bank," Locke said, shaking his head. "She works three times as hard as anyone there. And her latest project, getting her MBA from Harvard . . . I think it's too much for her. But Amber is driven, extremely intense. And I'm sure she didn't mean to be intentionally rude to you, Ashlee."

"I guess I'm not her idea of what her twin should be."

"I think it's more because you remind Amber that she is adopted. She wants so much to be an Aames by birth."

They had reached Ashlee's little orange Rabbit and she opened the car door and swung her suitcase out onto the ground. Locke caught a glimpse of the dolls on the backseat and lifted out a chubby baby boy dressed in a bright red snowsuit. The doll was the size of an actual one-year-old child. "Who's this little guy?"

Locke looked ridiculous holding that fat doll, and Ashlee had to laugh. "That's Locke, Junior, your long-lost son. Amber wasn't the only one I planned on surprising this trip."

Locke laughed too. "Ah, yes, he has the Aames nose. A striking resemblance." Next he removed a little-girl doll with blond pigtails and wearing a yellow gingham dress, pinafore, and Mary Janes. "This must be Ashlee, Junior. Is this how you looked as a child, Ashlee? A little angel with pigtails, a turned-up nose, and big brown eyes?"

"I was not a little angel." Ashlee slung her canvas tote over her shoulder and picked up her suitcase. "I was a holy terror. All the Martin kids were. I guess all you Aames kids were perfect?"

"Pretty much so, I'm afraid," Locke confessed with a smile.

"Poor Sharon and Brian. They seem like such regular kids. It must be hard for them to follow in the wake of paragons. Where is their mother, anyway? Alec didn't mention that she lived here."

"She doesn't." Locke frowned. "Three years ago Nancy said she found life in Aames stifling and ran away to New York City to find herself. Now she's a clerk in a bookshop and lives with a would-be artist in some warehouse loft. And claims she's never been happier," he added indignantly.

"And the kids stayed here with their father," Ashlee observed.

"They don't fit in with Nancy's new life. At least my parents are here to give them some stability." Locke sighed. "Nancy and Bryce's divorce really shook the family. They seemed an ideal match. Same background and upbringing, same values, or so we thought."

"People change. Maybe Nancy really *was* stifled. If Bryce had followed her to New York and tried to help make changes . . ."

"You sound like a pop psychologist out of one of those ungodly best sellers that proliferate on the market. Do you advocate a woman leaving her children, wrecking a perfectly good marriage to—"

"I'd never leave my children," Ashlee said calmly. "And I believe in working hard to make a marriage last, but the man has to work at it too. It has to be a mutual give-and-take. If I were married with kids, my husband would have to contribute more to our lives than a paycheck and his honorable family name."

"Marriage today!" Locke snorted. "Everyone has different expectations but no one bothers to compare notes before rushing blindly to the altar. By then it's too late. Next come the inevitable disappointments and the arguments and the accusations. I certainly made the right choice when I decided to make my profession my life. Alec's and Bryce's divorces confirmed it for me."

"You prefer physics to women," Ashlee said speculatively.

"You've misinterpreted me, Ashlee. I've chosen physics over marriage. Women do have a place in my life, but not a wife. I'm a confirmed bachelor."

Ashlee bit back a retort. If he only knew. Lord, she wished *she* didn't! "Here." She tossed him the remaining doll, a soft-sculpture witch complete with wart and crooked nose, tall pointed black hat, broomstick, and cat. It was an original Ashlee design and one of Creativity's most popular items. "You can carry Witch Hazel."

"You have some interesting traveling companions." Locke studied the doll, admiring it for a moment before he took Ashlee's suitcase and tote and handed the dolls to her in exchange. "Did you bring them all the way from North Carolina?"

"I thought Amber might like them. But I guess she doesn't like dolls, does she?"

"She never has, much to Mother's dismay. From the time she was tiny Amber rejected all and any little-girl-type things in favor of trying to excel in whatever we boys were doing."

They walked to the house and Ashlee felt a wave of sadness sweep through her. Even as children she and Amber had been different: Amber striving to excel and be perfect like the Aameses, Ashlee playing and raising Cain and being an utterly typical kid like her Martin cousins.

"I think it's fortunate that you came here, Ashlee." Locke's voice intruded upon her thoughts. "You could be very good for Amber, you know."

Ashlee glanced sharply at him. "I know you think that I've been hurt and it's kind of you to try to make amends, but you don't have to bother. I'm not the sensitive type who is crushed by a few harsh words. I'm tough, like all of the Martins, so please don't try to placate me with—"

"I'm not trying to placate you, Ashlee. I meant what I said. Amber could certainly use a few sisterly tips on—uh—the art of being feminine. Dressing and hair styles and makeup. How to act more—um—womanly around men."

Ashlee stopped dead and stared at him, not quite sure he was really saying what she thought he was saying. "And you think I'm just that sort of woman who can teach her the dimwitted little feminine tricks of the trade?" she said tightly.

"Ashlee, I was complimenting you, not insulting you."

"It didn't sound that way from here, Mr. Aames."

"Doctor," Locke corrected patiently. "I'm not a medical doctor, but I use the title because I—"

"I understand all about Ph.D.s," Ashlee growled.

"Good for you!" Locke smiled at her as if she were a particularly stupid student who'd finally grasped the concept of adding two plus two. Ashlee's eyes glittered, and she began to count to ten. "Ashlee, perhaps I didn't express myself clearly about helping out Amber, but I really do believe you can. You're pretty and you're sexy and you know how to"—he paused, assessing her thoughtfully—"to act around men. What to say, how to use your eyes, how to move. Body language is the term, I believe."

Ashlee made it to seven and abandoned the count. "Are you trying to say that I know how to come on to a man?" She snatched her suitcase from his hand and ripped the tote from his shoulder. "That I'm so good at it, I can give lessons? May I ask how you've arrived at your conclusion?"

"The way any capable scientist reaches a conclusion," Locke said. "From careful observation." He tried to take the suitcase back, but Ashlee hung on to it.

"Are you implying that I came on to you?" she asked, thoroughly enraged. Managing to balance her luggage and all three dolls, Ashlee stormed toward the house.

"I didn't mind," Locke said, easily keeping pace with her, his voice maddeningly calm. "In fact, I'll even admit it. I'm attracted to you, Ashlee."

Ashlee stomped up the two wide steps to the front porch. "Am I supposed to be thrilled?" Her temper, always on the volatile side, flamed into full fury. What a perfectly rotten day this had turned out to be. Her twin was totally out of it and now this irritating, condescending Yankee had the nerve to accuse her of coming on to him. "Well, I'm not! And I wasn't flirting with you and I'm not attracted to you and"—her voice rose defiantly—"I'm certainly not going to marry you!"

Three

"I'm crushed," Locke said dryly. "Although I don't recall asking you."

Ashlee was horrified. She thought her face must be a deep shade of purple. She'd passed mere red the moment she blurted out her foolish precognitive flash. There was no way to recover her lost dignity; her only way out of this mortifying scene was to disappear. Which she did with incredible swiftness. Keeping a death grip on her belongings, Ashlee was inside the house and up the stairs before Locke could utter another word.

Unaware of the humiliating front-porch scene, Sharon showed Ashlee to her room, the promised yellow one with adjacent bath on the second floor. Ashlee glanced around at the faded yellow roses on the wallpaper, the polished wood floor with its small Oriental rug, the plain white chenille bedspread. The room was sparsely furnished with a double bed, highboy, and small nightstand. The wood was dark, depressingly so, Ashlee thought. One tiny watercolor seascape graced the walls. The best bedroom in the house, Locke had said. Ashlee visualized her own small apartment in Chapel Hill, with its colorful walls and posters and quilts, the warm comfortable furniture and burnt-orange wall-to-wall carpeting. Yankees had peculiar tastes, she decided.

"This doll is adorable!" Sharon squealed, picking up the baby boy in the snowsuit.

"You can have him." Ashlee pressed her hands against her cheeks to cool them. They were still flaming with embarrassment. She'd done a spectacular job of making a fool of herself.

"Can I really?" Sharon was thrilled. "Thanks, Ashlee. I've never seen such a cute doll. Where did you get it?"

"I made it." Ashlee closed her eyes, and Locke's amused grin flashed before her. Instantly her eyes snapped open. "I make dolls and other crafts for the gift shop a friend and I own in Chapel Hill. That's the town where the University of North Carolina is located," she added with a touch of native pride.

"You don't work in a gas station?" Sharon sounded disappointed. "You're not a waitress at a truck-stop diner?"

"Sometimes, when I go back to visit my family and if they're short-handed there, I help out. But it's not my full-time occupation. And you don't have to tell your family," Ashlee continued fiercely. "Let them believe that I'm some sort of moronic Daisy Mae. They seem to want to."

Sharon nodded. "I won't breathe a word. Want to come up to my room and see it? I have it fixed up real neat."

"Maybe later, Sharon. I think I'd like to take a shower now."

"My room is on the third floor. Come up anytime, Ashlee." The girl rushed over to give Ashlee a quick hug. "Thanks for the doll and—and I'm really glad you're here."

Ashlee watched Sharon race out of the room, the

doll in her arms. What a shame that Sharon wasn't her long-lost little sister; they were already in harmonic accord. Should she be depressed that the only Aames on her wavelength was just thirteen years old? And ten. She'd hit it off with Brian too.

Sighing, Ashlee walked into the bathroom and stifled a groan of dismay. There was no shower, only a very old porcelain bathtub. And the little room was icy cold, its only source of heat a white radiator that was turned off. The thin postage-stamp-size bathmat was no protection against the coldness of the floor. Ashlee turned on the water and began to undress. And these were considered luxury accommodations? The Aameses weren't merely Yankees, they were Spartans as well. Would she and Amber ever find a common ground?

Wrapped in her bright aquamarine velour bathrobe and with matching slippers on her feet. Ashlee began to unpack. The room was warmer; she had turned on the radiators and they were hissing with heat. The small closet and the drawers in the highboy were empty, and she transferred her clothes from the suitcases as she thought about Amber. How could she reach her sister if her very existence symbolized what Amber most wanted to forget? That she was not a full-blooded Aames by birth, but the child they had adopted. Had Amber ever wondered about their biological mother? And the man who had fathered her? Obviously not. She had been too concerned with keeping up with the Aameses.

There was a tap on the door and it was opened before Ashlee could utter a sound. Locke Aames stood on the threshold. "I didn't realize that you weren't dressed," he said, his gaze traveling over her as she stood at the window, the robe clinging to the soft curves of her figure.

For a split second Ashlee was confused. She'd

been so preoccupied with her thoughts that she felt strangely suspended between two worlds. It all came back as she felt Locke's gaze upon her. The man she was fated to marry, the man who had suggested she give her sister lessons in stereotypical, imbecilic feminine flirting. Because she was such a pro in the sport.

"Still mad at me?" Locke grinned, entering the room and closing the door behind him.

He appeared vividly in her mind's eye as he walked toward her, but he wasn't wearing the green sweater and wool slacks. In her mind picture he was dressed in formal attire and she stood beside him wearing a wedding dress of antique lace, a dress she had never seen before. She knew at once it was an Aames possession, a wedding gown worn by all Aames brides. Ashlee pressed her fingers to her temples and considered the benefits of a frontal lobotomy.

"Are you all right?" Locke asked with concern.

Ashlee shook her head, then gave a quick nod. The scene had been so vivid, it was weird to find themselves here, in this faded room. "Just . . ." She tried to find some appropriate response.

"Just?" Locke prompted.

Ashlee sighed. "Mentally drained."

Locke's face softened. "Of course you are. And if it's any consolation, Amber isn't as cool as she pretended to be. She's been quite shaken by your appearance."

"I wanted her to be happy, not shaken. Can I see her now? Does she want to talk to me?"

"Her date is here and she's downstairs. I suggested that we all go out to dinner tonight—Bryce and his date, Alec, Cynthia, Amber and her date, and me. I've come to invite you to join us."

What an odious, unappealing idea. Ashlee flopped down on the bed. "No thanks. Y'all run along without me."

"I think you should come with us, Ashlee."

Ashlee shook her head. "I'll stay here with the kids.

"I *want* you to come with us, Ashlee." Locke was standing beside the bed. "With me," he added huskily.

He was going to kiss her. Ashlee read the intent in his gray-green eyes. And she could react one of two ways: refuse or let him kiss her. On the negative side, they were in a bedroom and she was sitting on the bed wearing only a robe. But on the other hand, there were a half dozen other people in the house and Locke would hardly ravish her moments before taking her out to dinner with his family. In fact, Locke didn't strike her as the type to ravish anyone anywhere. Whoever heard of a passionate thermodynamic physicist? Locke was too cerebral, too controlled, too reserved a Yankee to light any fires.

He took both her hands in his and pulled her to her feet. Ashlee made her decision; she would let him kiss her. Her sense of humor, like her temper, was quick to surface, and she couldn't suppress a smile. Not even a Victorian maiden begrudged a kiss to the man she was to marry.

"You have an enchanting smile," Locke said softly, gazing down into her eyes. Ashlee didn't bother to mention that the smile was for her own private joke, not for him. She found herself intrigued by the gold flecks in his eyes and by the way the corners of his mouth tilted into a smile. He had a mesmerizing smile, far more potent than his brother Alec's practiced flashes. His lips were well-shaped, sensual. . . . She hadn't noticed that before. Seemingly of its own volition, her forefinger traced the outline of his lips. "So do you."

Locke laughed huskily. "That's the first time I've ever been told that." His arms encircled her and he drew her closer. Ashlee's heart began to beat with unexpected anticipation. She really wanted him to kiss her, she realized to her own surprise. She watched his face come closer, studying his mouth, wondering how it would feel pressed against hers.

"Then the Yankee women are blind," she murmured, "because you do have a beautiful smile. Inviting." She slipped her arms slowly around his neck and the action brought her against his hard, solid body. "Intriguing. Sexy."

"I was going to say the same thing about yours," Locke said, his lips touching hers as he spoke. The kiss began softly, tentatively, his mouth brushing lightly over hers, then lingering longer and increasing the pressure. His hands roamed over her back, molding the soft velour against her skin, pressing her closer until her breasts were crushed against his chest.

Ashlee's fingers stroked his neck, running through the dark thickness of his hair. She drew her head back slightly and gazed up at him drowsily. "Hmmm. Not bad."

Locke's eyes snapped open wide. "What?"

"I've never kissed a genius before. Or a physicist, or a Yankee, for that matter. That's sort of a triple whammy, I'd have said. I wasn't expecting much, but as far as kisses go, it wasn't bad at all."

Locke's jaw dropped and he gaped at her, his expression changing swiftly from incredulous to indignant to unexpected humor. "You little brat." He gave a mock growl. "I haven't even begun to show you how proficient we Yankee genius physicists are in the art of kissing. Your Southern gentlemen and good ole boys aren't even in the competition."

Ashlee raised her eyebrows skeptically, then spoiled the effect by grinning. "All right, Dr. Aames. I'm ready for round two."

He didn't quite know how to take her. Ashlee could read the confusion in his eyes. And there was something else there as well, a strange combination of fascination and determination. She had challenged him, however jokingly, and he had decided to take up the gauntlet.

This time he took her mouth without hesitation, his lips warm and commanding, his tongue flicking at the corners of her lips, cajoling and teasing, determined to arouse her. His large hands moved unceasingly, smoothing over her back, over the curve of her hips, molding her into the strong masculine planes of his body.

And suddenly, quite unexpectedly, Ashlee caught fire. Her lips parted and his tongue penetrated the moist softness of her mouth and rubbed against her tongue in a seductive, caressive rhythm. Something inside her went weak and soft, and she inhaled on a sigh. Locke's palms stroked along her spine, then moved slowly over her rib cage to rest just below the undersides of her breasts. He deepened the kiss as his hands slipped between the lapels of her robe and cupped one soft, full breast. Ashlee shuddered with a tiny, muffled moan of pleasure.

Locke lifted his head for a split second to gaze down at her closed eyes, her flushed cheeks, and softly swollen lips. A small smile of satisfaction flickered across his face before his mouth closed over hers once more.

Her senses reeling, Ashlee allowed her tongue to dart into his mouth and rub seductively against his. Her finger stroked the strong column of his neck and feathered through the thick hair above his collar. Their breathing quickened, grew heavier as the kiss intensified with passionate urgency.

"Ashlee," Locke murmured, his voice low with passion. He caressed her breast possessively, one long finger finding the taut nipple as he thrust his thigh between hers. The pressure was an exquisite pleasure, and Ashlee strained closer, wanting more. She felt Locke loosen the tie belt of her robe to slip the garment from her shoulders. She was naked beneath the robe and the probable results of such an action filtered slowly through her passion-drugged senses to an alert little corner of her mind.

"Locke . . . No." Ashlee's voice was as husky as Locke's. He replaced the robe slowly, reluctantly, and folded her into his arms, cradling her tightly against him. She lay against him, stunned by the force of her own arousal. How had it happened? One moment she had been clearly enjoying a rather pleasant kiss, the next . . . she had seemed to ignite and explode in his arms. She could hear the heavy thudding of Locke's heart beneath her ear, feel his blatant masculine arousal against her hips, and a compulsive shiver of desire pulsed through her.

Locke's lips brushed the top of her head. "This reminds me a little of one of my early experiments with my first chemistry set," he murmured in a deep voice. "The results were a totally unexpected spontaneous combustion."

He was playing it light and Ashlee knew she should follow his lead and toss in a clever little quip of her own. Except the situation had lost its humor for her. These moments in Locke's arms had given her a glimpse of something she had never before experienced, something that beckoned and tempted with seductive allure. Something danger-ous because she couldn't have it, and Ashlee knew that the sure route to misery was wanting the unattainable. She'd picked up enough psychology from her years of testing to be aware of that fact. She had come here to find her twin sister, not to indulge in a hopeless affair with Locke Aames. An affair between two such polar opposites could only be an all-out disaster for all concerned. Ashlee took stock of the situation and took hold of herself. She was here to win Amber's love, not to arouse Locke's lust. She moved out of Locke's arms, a frozen little smile on her face.

"Ashlee?" He reached for her and she neatly sidestepped him. His smile faded. "What's wrong?"

"What could possibly be wrong?" she said brightly.

"I don't know, that's why I'm asking. I do know that you suddenly went stiff and pulled away from me and that now your face looks like a thundercloud despite that saccharine tone of yours."

"The scientist presents his hypothesis, listing his observations as he searches for a logical conclusion," Ashlee said mockingly. "But this time he's going to be dead-ended because the premise of his theory is false. Sorry to foil you, Locke, but there is absolutely nothing wrong."

"How do you know so much about the scientific method?" Locke asked curiously.

Ashley turned away from him and thought of the countless experiments in the parapsychology labs in which she had taken part. She had listened and observed, too, and had absorbed quite a bit of information on the methods of obtaining empirical data. But to explain it all to Locke, who believed her to be on a par with the Beverly Hillbillies, hardly seemed worth the effort. "I heard it on a talk show on the idiot box," she said coldly.

Locke sighed impatiently and Ashlee looked back at him. He was staring at her, his arms folded across his chest, his legs apart in an aggressive stance. For some reason her irritation faded at the sight of his own. "Speaking of thunderclouds, you have a full-fledged hurricane brewing in *your* face."

"I'm trying to figure out what happened," he said. "I'm not usually so slow on the uptake, but I admit that you baffle me. We were holding each other and I know you wanted me as much as I wanted you when—wham! Not only do you put up these impenetrable barriers, but you deny that you've done it. What gives, Ashlee?"

"Maybe it's just my li'l ole feminine wiles at work.

You know, the ones you want me to teach to Amber?"

"Are you still angry about that? Ashlee, I was paying you a compliment!"

"That's what is known as a left-handed compliment in my book, Dr. Aames."

"Don't try to divert me, Ashlee. Your withdrawal had nothing to do with feminine wiles. I can see right through any phony little female ploy. I find them extremely transparent and tedious as well. You weren't—"

"Honey, when it comes to feminine wiles, your Yankee women aren't even in the competition with us Southern belles and mountain gals," Ashlee drawled, her eyes alight with mischief. "You may as well give up and concede now."

"Concede?" Locke was fighting back a smile. "No way. We Yankees won the war, remember?"

"Not the way I learned it."

Locke's smile broke through. "Can we agree on a truce for now? At least through dinner?"

Ashlee sighed. "So we're back to *that* again."

"You're coming with us, Ashlee." It wasn't quite a command, but not quite a question either. "Please," he tacked on, and promptly looked embarrassed. Apparently Locke Aames wasn't accustomed to pleading for company.

"Oh, all right," Ashlee agreed rather ungraciously. "You mentioned your brother and his date, Amber and her date, you and Cynthia and Alec. I take it I'm Alec's date for the evening?"

"No. You're mine."

"What about Cynthia?"

"She's Alec's date."

"How did that happen?" Ashlee grinned. "I was ordered to whip up a little snack for the two of you, remember?"

She had the satisfaction of seeing a dark red flush stain his face. "I've already apologized for mistaking your true identity. As for Cynthia, she's quite happy to be with Alec." Locke's mouth twisted into a cynical sneer. "Cynthia is a professional husband-hunter. Any available Aames brother will do."

"So ultimately she'll wind up with none of the Aames brothers because no man wants what he can so easily have." Ashlee laughed. "Don't these Yankee mamas teach their daughters anything?"

Locke stood transfixed, staring at her, captivated by her smile, her dimples, her dancing brown eyes. He moved toward her, just managing to brush her cheek with his fingertips before she artfully darted away. "If you want me to come with you, you'll have to leave now. I must get dressed."

"I don't suppose you'd let me stay and watch?" Locke's tone was hopeful.

"Sorry." She caught his arm and pulled him to the door. "You'll have to earn that privilege." With a cheeky grin she pushed him into the hall, closed the door, and locked it, laughing out loud when he muttered a dark, sexy threat as he rattled the doorknob.

Although she hadn't brought anything very dressy, Ashlee did have a few skirts she thought might be appropriate for tonight's miserable little group date. She chose an ultrasuede pink skirt and vest with a pewter, pink, and purple striped blouse, pink stockings, and gray strappy sandals. She liked the three and a half inches the thin heels added to her small five-foot-four frame, but as she viewed herself in the bathroom mirror, Ashlee felt a moment's trepidation. Amber's shoes had been so orthopedic, the antithesis of these frothy gray confections. And she was depressingly certain that her sister had never worn these colors in her life, nor ultrasuede. Amber was undoubtedly against manmade fibers; she would be the one-hundred-percent-wool-or-cotton type.

"Neat outfit!" Sharon said enthusiastically when she entered the yellow bedroom. "I wish I had one like it."

Uh-oh, Ashlee thought. Would an outfit that appealed to a thirteen-year-old be out of place among the women in the group? She'd already seen Cynthia's tasteful burgundy tea dress and knew the styles would clash. With Sharon's whole-hearted approval, Ashlee affixed medium-sized gold hoops to her earlobes and pulled a handful of her hair into a loose topknot. The rest of her hair tumbled to her shoulders in its usual stubborn straightness.

Sharon and Brian accompanied Ashlee down-stairs to what they called the parlor, where the men were sipping port, the women dry sherry. Intro-ductions were made. Bryce Aames, the oldest brother, was a combination in looks of Locke and Alec, possessing the strong Aames chin and jaw and intent gray-green eyes. His date, Lori Charles-ton, looked all of nineteen and was wearing tight jeans and an equally tight sweater, and seemed an odd choice of companion for the conservatively dressed banker nearly twice her age. Bryce's answer to his ex-wife's artist-in-the-loft? Ashlee noticed that Sharon and Brian gave their father and his date a wide berth.

Ashlee smiled hopefully at Amber, praying, will-ing her to return the smile. But the polite little gri-mace that Amber managed didn't reach her eyes, which were glued to the brilliant pink of Ashlee's skirt and vest. Ashlee viewed her twin's clothes with similar dismay. Amber had traded the severe suit for a shapeless black wool dress, one Ashlee wouldn't have even worn to a funeral, let alone a dinner date. It had a round collar, long sleeves, and a straight skirt, and was too long and too dreary to flatter even a world-renowned beauty. And black was simply the wrong color for their mutual com-plexion and coloring; Ashlee had known that for years. She happened to catch Locke's eye and knew that he had been watching her. Worse, she knew that he knew exactly what her reaction to her sister's dress had been.

An uncomfortable combination of disloyalty and guilt shot through her. Who was she to pronounce fashion judgment? So she and her sister had different tastes in clothes. That wasn't uncommon in sisters who had been raised together. Since when was she, Ashlee Martin, a style expert? Perhaps Amber's tastes were attractive to her circle. She had a date, didn't she? And he seemed to be a nice enough man.

Amber's date was Garrison Kramer, who Alec mentioned worked in the Cambridge branch of the Aames bank. He was tall and blond with friendly blue eyes and seemed genuinely excited by the sudden appearance of Amber's twin. He welcomed Ashlee warmly, perhaps a little too warmly, for Amber attached herself to his arm and glared when Garrison exclaimed for the sixth time how great it was that the twins had found each other. When he marveled at the stunning difference in their appearance, Amber suggested in icy tones that it was time to leave for the restaurant.

"Where are we going?" Ashlee asked Amber, trying yet again to win a positive response.

"To a new Japanese restaurant that opened recently in Boston," Amber replied with all the warmth of a bored tour guide.

Ashlee took a deep breath. "That sounds interesting. I've never had Japanese food. Have you, Amber?"

"Yes."

Ashlee conceded that her smile was growing a bit strained, but she tried once more. "Is it good? Do you like it?"

"Yes," replied the loquacious Amber, turning away from her.

"Let's take two cars, no sense everyone driving,"

Alec suggested. His arm was around Cynthia's waist, she didn't seem to mind the sudden switch in Aames brothers. And she hadn't glared once at Ashlee since her arrival in the parlor. Ashlee's opinion of her rose. Cynthia seemed to learn from her mistakes.

Ashlee wanted to go in the same car as Amber. She was desperate to talk to her sister, to break through the wall Amber had so quickly erected. She turned to Locke, a plea in her eyes.

"Can Ashlee and I ride with you, Gar?" Locke asked casually, and Ashlee's heart leaped with gratitude. He had understood and was trying to help her.

"We've already arranged to go with Alec and Cynthia," Amber said quickly. There was a momentary silence that threatened to stretch into an embarrassing one until Locke spoke up. "Then I'll drive and Bryce and Lori can go with us."

Ashlee suppressed the urge to scream with frustration. There were too many people in this house. Amber could hide among them indefinitely at this rate. The whole evening promised to be a failure in her quest to know her sister. They were riding in separate cars, the whole group would be present at the restaurant. . . . Ashlee's spirits flagged. When Locke tucked her hand into the crook of his arm and guided her from the room, she made no protest, but cast a longing glance over her shoulder at her twin. Amber wasn't even looking her way; she was talking with Garrison Kramer, her thin face displaying the first signs of animation that Ashlee had seen since her arrival.

Locke steered his navy and beige Oldsmobile along the dark road, only the classical music from the tape deck breaking the silence within the car. Bryce and Lori were necking in the backseat. Ashlee had turned to make polite conversation and found them kissing passionately, Bryce's hand firmly cupping Lori's breast. Ashlee grimaced.

Heavy necking in the backseat of a car with another couple in the front seat struck her as excessively adolescent, but she should have predicted it. It was going to be that kind of evening.

"You're not very talkative," Locke said, reaching for her hand. He carried it to his thigh and covered it with his own. Ashlee debated over protesting the possessive gesture, but decided not to bother. She was in no mood for the sparring match that would inevitably follow. And in a strange way she felt that Locke was her ally, the only one she had in the Aames family apart from the children. And he was definitely the only one she could question about her twin. Ashlee was hungry to know more about her sister, and Locke could supply some essential information.

"How long has Amber been dating Garrison Kramer? Are they serious? Have they known each other long? How did they meet?" She fired the questions like a series of volleys and felt Locke's muscles tense beneath her hand.

"You seem quite interested in Garrison Kramer," he said in a tone that was too casual, too silky. "But then, he was clearly quite impressed with you too."

"Just what is that crack supposed to mean?" Ashlee pulled her hand back as if she'd been stung. Just when she'd begun to feel that Locke might be on her side, he had to make a nasty insinuation like that.

"Just a little friendly advice, honey. Turn down the feminine wiles when dealing with Garrison Kramer. You won't win any points with Amber by bowling him over with your charm. She's secretly admired him for months and this is only their third date."

"Wiles?" Ashlee simmered. "I was just being polite and friendly to the man."

"Ashlee, when a sexy little blond with a smile

like yours turns it on, a man doesn't think in terms of polite and friendly."

"Oh!" Her simmer reached a boil. "Not again! You're accusing me of coming on to him, aren't you? First to you, then to my own sister's date."

The music shifted to a dramatic piano concerto and Ashlee's voice rose along with it. "Is it just you or all physicists or all Yankees? Can't a woman smile and be friendly to a man without it being interpreted as a come-on? Do I have to wear a sign or something? 'Not interested, Just Polite.' " Her anger spilled out like Sharon's boiled-over pudding. The man infuriated her. "Stop the car at once. I'm getting out!"

"Ashlee, don't be ridiculous. You can't—"

"If you don't stop, I swear I'll open the door and jump out. I know how. We used to practice jumping out of cars in the field when my cousin Albie first got his license."

"You—you're not serious, are you?" Locke cast her a quick, uncertain glance.

"Of course I'm serious about jumping out of Albie's car. It seemed like a useful skill to learn at the time, although I admit I've never had the urge to put it to use until right now."

Locke frowned, then smiled, then frowned again. "Are you *really* serious? I can never tell with you. You say some of the strangest things."

"There's never any question about you," Ashlee retorted. "You're always serious, aren't you? So serious that one doesn't dare smile without you looking for some hidden sexual motive."

Locke cleared his throat, was silent a moment, then cleared his throat again. "Ashlee, if I was wrong about you—er—flirting with Kramer—"

"Which you were!"

"Then I apologize. But I'm not wrong about Amber being jealous over Kramer's reaction to you, Ashlee. I was watching her and I saw the way she felt. Hell, I know the way I—" He broke off abruptly and tightened his fingers around the steering wheel. "Just tone down the charm to be on the safe side, Ashlee. Or"—he gave a husky, self-mocking laugh—"make those smiles of yours just for me."

"One would almost think *you* were jealous," Ashlee said sharply, still burning over his unwarranted accusations. That notion was preposterous, of course, but she wondered if Locke might be right about Amber's jealousy. She'd been so cold and she certainly hadn't shared Garrison's enthusiasm for her long-lost twin. Ashlee began to gnaw at her thumbnail, a deplorable habit she was certain she'd kicked. It was ironic, really. She had never been the type other women found threatening. Since childhood she'd gotten along splendidly with members of her own sex. Why did her own twin sister have to be the first female to take exception to her? The second, she corrected herself. Cynthia was no fan of hers either. Perhaps she was fated to rub all Yankee women the wrong way. Her shoulders slumped with discouragement and she gnawed her nail harder.

And then she saw it, clear as a photograph before her eyes. "Do we pass an intersection with a little lane off to the left?" she asked suddenly. "There's a big oak tree and a hedge just beyond a stop sign."

"That sounds like Merrill's Crossing, about a mile and a quarter down the road," Locke said.

"Well, you'd better slow down. You're going forty-five and the sign says the speed limit is only thirty. And there's a police car parked right in that little lane I mentioned."

"No one goes thirty on this road," Locke said, scoffing. "And unlike the Carolinas, Aames doesn't have speed traps with patrol cars lurking in the bushes."

"You'd better slow down," Ashlee warned. "You're going to get a ticket."

"Honey, if you want to be a backseat driver, kindly climb into the backseat."

"But—"

"Ashlee, I don't appreciate being nagged about my driving. I'm not speeding recklessly. A thirty-mile speed limit on this road is ridiculous and—"

"Why don't you tell it to the policeman?" Ashlee suggested in honeyed tones. "He just motioned you over."

The flashing red light of the police car was visible in the rearview mirror. "Damn!" Locke clenched his teeth as he pulled over to the side of the road. The uniformed policeman approached the car and Locke rolled down the window.

"I clocked you at forty-five," the officer said politely. "May I see your driver's license and your car registration?" Locke handed the cards to the officer without a word.

"Aren't you going to tell him that the thirty-mile-an-hour speed limit is ridiculous?" Ashlee whispered, her face the picture of innocence. "And that the only speed traps are in the Carolinas?"

"Oh, shut up," Locke grumbled.

Ashlee completely failed to suppress a grin of amusement. A moment later Locke was smiling too.

Four

Ten minutes later, with a sixty-dollar speeding ticket in the glove compartment, the Oldsmobile was again heading toward Boston. At thirty miles per hour.

"Ashlee, how did you know the police car was there?" Bryce asked. He and Lori had surfaced for air shortly before the police officer had summoned the car over. "You told Locke about it before Merrill's Crossing was even in sight."

"Probably passed it on her way to the house," Locke surmised. "I should have listened to you, Ashlee. I will, next time."

"I didn't pass it. I've never been in this part of Aames," Ashlee said, glancing assessingly at Locke. Telling him about her psi ability on top of a sixty-dollar speeding ticket didn't seem like the best of timing. It would probably be better to wait for a more auspicious moment. "A—um—lucky guess, I suppose."

"You didn't sound like you were guessing. You sounded positive about it," Lori said. "It was like you *knew* a cop was there. Like you were psychic or something."

"Oh, right! She's psychic, that definitely explains it." Locke chuckled. "Why didn't I think of that?"

"You don't believe in clairvoyance?" Ashlee asked tentatively, and Locke laughed out loud. "That occult nonsense? Of course not! What rational, thinking person does?"

"I do," piped up Lori.

"I rest my case," Locke murmured in a voice so low only Ashlee could hear. She shifted uncomfortably.

"I really do believe in psychic phenomena," Lori said forcefully. "This semester I'm taking a course in parapsychology."

"Wouldn't something like basket weaving or ceramics be a little more useful?" Bryce teased.

"Parapsychology happens to be an accredited branch of psychology," Ashlee said. "And many well-known universities do experiments involving psychic phenomena. Dr. Ian Cameron is a Ph.D. at Duke University and he's become internationally renowned for his parapsychology experiments and articles. Likewise Dr. Stevenson at the University of Virginia." They were two men she admired and respected. Dr. Cameron was almost like another uncle to her and she felt honor-bound to defend their field. "There are many others, even at your precious Harvard."

"Bryce and Alec's precious Harvard," Locke said cheerfully. "I broke with Aames tradition and went to M.I.T., and I can assure you we have no magicians and charlatans on the staff there."

"Not all scientists scorn the field of parapsychology," Ashlee countered. Most, but not all. Dr. Cameron had once allowed a visiting group of atomic engineers to observe her tests. And they had been believers.

"Come on, Ashlee, you don't really believe in that ESP rubbish?"

He'd backed her against the wall with that one. Unless she blatantly lied, which she was loath to do, she had no choice but to tell him.

"It's not rubbish. The field of parapsychology has two main branches: ESP, or extra-sensory perception, which includes clairvoyance, telepathy, and precognition, and psychokinesis."

"Psychokinesis." Bryce chuckled. "That's when Carrie types bring down buildings with their psychic powers, isn't it?"

"That was pure fiction. Lab tests for psychokinesis generally involve the use of dice or revolving random patterns," Ashlee said coolly.

"You're really into this too," Lori exclaimed with enthusiasm. "Have you ever been tested for psi ability, Ashlee?"

Bryce and Locke's chuckles echoed in her ears as she said, "Yes, I have."

Locke stopped laughing. "You don't mean to say you've actually been involved with that junk? That voodoo trash?"

"You make it sound tawdry, like some kind of weird black magic, which it's not," Ashlee protested. "I've been tested by university professors under formal laboratory conditions. The results have been published in journals all over the world."

"Everybody knows that the methods of testing in that pseudo-field are highly unreliable and the test results are faked," Locke countered with a patronizing smile. "But a naive young girl from a small mountain town with all its inherent superstitions would be an ideal candidate for those quacks. You'd tend to believe and go along with anything they suggested, accept the subliminal coaching they would provide and—"

"That's not true!" Ashlee and Lori chorused.

"Why don't we simply agree to disagree on the subject of ESP?" Bryce suggested in a condescending tone that equalled Locke's. Ashlee saw red. Perhaps it was time for a little show-and-tell? But what could be a convincing display? Lori supplied the answer.

"Here." She thrust a ring into Ashlee's hand. "We did this in class when a psychic visited. Ashlee will give me the impressions she receives from this ring using her clairvoyant powers."

Ashlee never participated in such glitzy, theatrical displays, but tonight she decided to make an exception. The Aames brothers were so smug, so patronizing. She was determined at least to challenge their stubborn resistance to the existence of psi. She held Lori's ring and allowed the pictures to wash over her mind. "The original owner of this ring is dead. She was a woman. . . . I see something blue, something which is associated closely with this ring."

"Incredible!" cried Lori excitedly. "The ring was my grandmother's and she died seven years ago. And the something blue closely associated with the ring is a little blue Delft porcelain cow which Grandma used as a ringholder. I have the little cow in my room and I use it for the same purpose."

Ashlee handed the ring back to Lori, who regarded her with admiration and awe. "I've never met Ashlee until tonight," Lori said to Bryce in an I-told-you-so manner. "So how could she know about my grandmother's ring and the Delft cow if she weren't clairvoyant?"

"May I offer a more scientific, realistic answer to this so-called miracle?" Locke asked, and proceeded without an answer. "The ring is obviously a woman's antique ring, so it would be a safe bet that the original owner was both female and dead. Ashlee didn't say it was your *grandmother's* ring, Lori, you did. Nor did she mention the Delft cow. She gave some vague answer about something blue being associated with it. Another safely oblique answer. A true believer could come up with anything that might work with the blue connection."

"Maybe Grandma wore it with a blue dress," suggested Bryce entering in on the spirit of the game. "As the stone is blue, that would be a feasible connection. "Maybe the sky was blue when she wore it or a blue jay flew by. There are endless possibilities."

"You told us about the porcelain cow, Lori, not Ashlee," Locke pointed out.

"But why would I want to pretend that I'm clairvoyant if I'm not?" Ashlee asked wearily. "Do you think I do it for attention? I don't, I assure you. I've never sold predictions to the tabloids or tried mindreading tricks on TV. I've helped people when I could, but I've never used my gift for profit or—"

"How did you score on the card tests, Ashlee?" Lori interrupted.

"I've consistently scored between eighteen and twenty-one ever since I was six," Ashlee replied quietly.

"Wow!" Lori gasped.

"Another impressive feat?" mocked Locke. "Fill me in on this one."

"The card tests were originated by J. B. Rhine at Duke University in the '30s," Lori explained. "It's a controlled experiment for psi and involves a special deck of cards with five different designs on them. The cards are laid facedown and the subject, someone like Ashlee, writes down on a record sheet what symbol she thinks is on the card. At the end of a twenty-five-card run, the results are checked against the target deck."

"The law of chance expects five correct hits," Ashlee added. "Anything significantly above is considered an indicator of psi ability."

"Eleven or twelve is considered quite high," Lori said admiringly. "Your score must have sent them over the moon, Ashlee. Particularly as they were consistent."

Ashlee recalled the excitement in the lab when her test results were revealed time after time, the apprehension when she was retested, and the subsequent elation when she continued to perform with astonishing accuracy. Yes, Dr. Cameron and the others had been "over the moon." She was giving proof to theories, substance to dissertations.

"Maybe Ashlee can get in touch with our uncle Charlie," Locke suggested jovially. He obviously was still treating the whole matter as one huge joke. "Uncle Charlie died about ten years ago, and we've never been able to locate his golden guineas. He had a dozen gold coins from the era of George III of England that had been passed down in the family over the years. My brothers and I were supposed to inherit them, but they've never been found. Uncle Charlie got a little peculiar toward the end and hid them too well. We've searched the house from attic to cellar for them. Why don't you hold a seance, Ashlee, and conjure him up so we can ask him where the coins are? They're a priceless inheritance for future Aameses."

"I've always had a yen to chat with J. P. Morgan," Bryce said, chortling. "Call him up, too, Ashlee."

"And while you're at it, invite Albert Einstein to join us. I'd like to discuss a certain puzzling aspect of my latest research," Locke added. Both brothers laughed uproariously at their own wit.

"I'm not a medium," Ashlee retorted. Sandy had often expressed similar sentiments and jokes and she laughed them off. Why should it bother her that Locke refused to take her seriously?

"She is what is known as a sensitive," Lori said, seemingly oblivious to the mockery. "Mediums are able to communicate with spirits. Sensitives are those who are blessed with psi ability. A medium may be a sensitive, but sensitives are generally not considered mediums. I'm doing a paper on the subject," she added importantly.

"Damn!" Bryce snapped his fingers. "There go

Uncle Charlie's golden guineas. What a disappointment!"

"Well, if you can't conjure up spirits, maybe you can tell me who I was in my past life?" Locke teased. "Any vibes, Ashlee? Julius Caesar, perhaps? Peter the Great of Russia? I've always felt a particular affinity with Sir Isaac Newton. Could I . . . be he?"

Ashlee sniffed. "My guess is the village idiot." She was more than ready to drop the entire subject and wished that it had never come up in the first place. "I don't do past-life readings or conduct seances or bend spoons or read minds or play with the ouija board. I'm not a magician or a charlatan. I just know things. I don't know why or how."

"Maybe you were dropped on your head as a baby?" Locke said, grinning.

"Actually," Ashlee said seriously, "it was a blow to my head that seemed to trigger the whole thing. I was in the car accident that killed my foster parents when I was six years old. My skull was fractured and I was in a coma for two weeks."

"Oh, my God, Ashlee!" Locke was aghast. "I'm so sorry. I had no idea . . . When I made that flippant remark, I didn't know . . ."

Figuring he was suitably horrified by his gaffe, Ashlee said, "I know you were only teasing, Locke. I didn't take offense."

"This is the second time . . . First the maid, now this . . ." Locke mumbled. Ashlee wondered if this was the first time he had ever made an error. What had Sharon said about no one making mistakes in the Aames house? "I feel like such an insensitive clod," Locke said, groaning. "Please accept my apologies, Ashlee."

"Maybe if you grovel a little more," Ashlee teased. Locke appeared ready to take her at her word.

"Ashlee, I am so sorry—"

"I was only teasing!" Ashlee interjected swiftly. "Of course I accept your apology. You didn't know."

"Tell us what happened when you awoke from your coma," Lori said. She was hanging over the back of the front seat.

Ashlee glanced uncertainly at Locke. "Please continue," he said in a subdued tone. Ashlee was sorry she'd teased him; she really hadn't minded his jokes that much.

"When I came out of the coma the nurses in the hospital picked up on my—my abilities. I had no recollection of anything like it before. But when I described a plane crash at the Raleigh-Durham airport eight hours before it occurred, the parapsychologists at Duke were notified and they began a series of tests that seemed to confirm—" She decided not to say *psi ability* again.

"You've had those people messing around with your mind since you were six years old?" Locke seemed outraged on her behalf. "Right after your parents were killed? That's criminal!" His tone softened and he reached for her hand. "You poor kid. What a time you've had."

"I've been very happy," Ashlee protested. She would have snatched her hand away, but he held on to it. "My daddy's mother, my grandmother, took me in, and I was raised in a loving atmosphere with aunts and uncles and cousins all around." Privately she thought she had fared far better than Amber, who had been raised in the sterile atmosphere of Yankee excellence. "The only thing I've missed has been my twin sister, whom I've always known existed, years before I ever saw the birth certificate that proved it."

"And now you've found your sister." Lori sighed. "Does she have psi ability too?"

"No!" chorused Bryce and Locke too quickly. It was as if Lori had asked if Amber had lice! Ashlee frowned and removed her hand from Locke's.

Locke parked in a lot adjacent to the Japanese restaurant and Lori and Ashlee started to walk toward the building together. Bryce lingered behind with Locke.

"What a spacy chick!" Ashlee heard Bryce say in an aside not meant for her ears. Lori heard, too, and frowned. "Is he talking about you or me?" she whispered to Ashlee.

"I'll give you odds it's me," Ashlee said dryly, and Bryce's next remark proved her right.

"I don't think she should try that ESP nonsense on Amber," he said. "They're twins; who knows how Amber will react? And I'm worried about such a flaky type staying at the house. Sharon and Brian are impressionable children. I don't want their heads filled with this occult rubbish."

"Don't worry about it." A gust of wind carried Locke's voice to Ashlee, his words crystal-clear. "I'll handle her."

"Don't pay any attention to them," Lori whispered soothingly. "We both know how wrong they are."

But Ashlee's patience had reached its limits. First the heckling in the car, now Bryce's notion that she would be a bad influence on Amber, Sharon, and Brian. . . . Ashlee decided that she'd had it. Had she been a bellicose third-grader, she would have grabbed a handful of the Aames brothers' hair and hung on until they screamed for mercy. As an adult she had to settle for storming over to them and glowering, her hands on her hips.

"Tell me, Locke, how do you handle an undesirable weirdo like me? Burn me at the stake? That was a favorite with your ancestors up here in Massachusetts, wasn't it? And your level of tolerance is on a par with theirs."

"My brother and I were speaking confidentially," Bryce said, looking uncomfortable. Face-to-face confrontations were clearly not his style. Ashlee guessed he was the stab-in-the-back type, and she continued to glare. Bryce nervously shifted his gaze from hers and mumbled, "You weren't meant to hear what was said."

"I don't think you cared if I overheard or not; you just didn't want me to acknowledge that I had. I might be spacy, flaky, and weird, but I'm not a hypocrite." Ashlee's eyes flashed fire. "And I'm not about to walk into that restaurant with a phony smile pasted on my face and pretend that I don't know what you really think of me."

Several other people walking through the lot were beginning to stare. Bryce cringed. "Couldn't we—er—discuss this matter at some other time?" he whispered urgently as he eyed the curious spectators. "And at some other place?"

"Go inside with Lori, Bryce," Locke said. "Tell the others that we'll be along in a few minutes."

"I won't be along at all," contradicted Ashlee. "I'm taking a taxi back to your house and then checking into a motel."

"You'll do no such thing, Ashlee," Locke said calmly, motioning Bryce and Lori to leave. "Let's clear up this misunderstanding right now."

Bryce and Lori departed. Ashlee turned to Locke. "Is this an example of how well you can handle me?" she said caustically.

"Ashlee, one of the first things that anyone learns about my brother Bryce is that he is extremely opinionated, and unfortunately he never hesitates to express those opinions. He is also distrustful toward anyone he hasn't known since birth, which, as you might imagine, is the majority of people in this world. The third lesson involving Bryce is to pay him and his opinions no mind. He doesn't speak for anyone but himself, Ashlee."

"Your handling methods aren't working, Dr. Aames. I'm still furious, and I wouldn't stay in your creaky old family mansion if you begged me!"

"I have no intention of begging you, Ashlee. I intend to appeal to your common sense. Staying in a motel will be quite expensive; I doubt if you could afford more than a couple of nights. And I believe you know it will take more time than that to win Amber's friendship."

He had her there. Ashlee frowned. She wasn't ready yet to let the issue drop. "Then I'll—I'll just go home! Amber hates me and she probably always will. No amount of time is going to change that!"

"Suppose I called your bluff and told you to go?" Locke said, laughing slightly. "Wouldn't you be left with the proverbial egg on your face? I'm half tempted to do it just to watch you scramble to reverse yourelf."

He was so confident, so sure of himself—and her. What made it even worse was that he was absolutely right; she had no intention of leaving. But it wasn't fair that he should know it! How to shatter that maddening complacency of his? She acted on a flash of feminine insight. "And why should I stay where I'm not wanted? There are people who love me back home in North Carolina, people who don't think I'm a demented freak. My family and my friends and Steve"—Ashlee watched him carefully as she plunged in the imaginary dagger with true Martin style—"the man who wants to marry me."

"Marry you?" Locke echoed, the expression on his face a mixture of irritation and shock. He didn't like the idea of her marrying; Ashlee had known that he wouldn't. Whether by feminine intuition or the Martin go-for-the-jugular fighting instincts or the much-scorned telepathy, she wasn't sure. But she had known. And Locke clearly hated the idea that he did mind.

"What kind of man would let his fiancée take off alone on a thousand-mile wild goose chase to parts unknown to find an equally unknown twin?" Locke seemed to be growing angrier by the second. "And what kind of fiancée are you, flirting and kissing another man? And in the bedroom!"

"Aren't I the wicked one?" Ashlee laughed. "Jezebel and Delilah rolled into one, hmm? You're lucky I've decided to let you escape my diabolical clutches."

Locke stared at her for a moment and then shook his head. "You've done it again. I don't know if you're serious or if you're putting me on and laughing up your sleeve at me."

"Oh, rest assured I am laughing at you. You're such a . . . a . . ." She paused in her search for a suitable description and grinned at him.

"Predictable idiot?" supplied Locke. "Believe me, it's a new role for me. You somehow seem to be one step ahead of me and I'm not used to it."

"I remember that you've rated women a boring second place to physics."

"No one could ever accuse you of being boring, Ashlee." He stared at her thoughtfully. "Ashlee?"

"Yes?"

"I mentioned earlier that you said . . . some strange things."

"I remember."

"Well, you really outdid yourself with that ESP stuff. Were you just kidding? Going along with that nutty Lori for laughs?"

Ashlee shrugged and sighed. It was hopeless. "I don't think Lori is nutty. Although why she dates that stuffed-shirt brother of yours does make one question her taste."

"She's Bryce's girl-of-the-month." Locke grimaced. "He changes them like calendar pages since Nancy left. Ashlee, I have something I'd like to ask you."

Ashlee shivered as a blast of cold air filtered through her coat. She hoped he was going to ask her to reconsider and go into the restaurant. She had already decided that she would, in order to be with Amber, she assured herself. And she was hungry, starved! It had been many hours since her last meal.

"Are you really engaged to this—Steve—in North Carolina?"

"No." Ashlee shook her head. "We're not officially engaged."

"But he's asked you to marry him?"

She glanced at him, and what she saw in his eyes caused a sudden throb deep within the very core of her. "It's just a matter of time."

"Until he asks you? Or until you accept?"

Ashlee hardly heard him. She hadn't given Steve a thought since leaving Chapel Hill. And now her mind was filled with the tantalizing memory of Locke's kiss, of the way he had touched her and the pulse-pounding feelings he had evoked within her.

Locke moved closer and laid his large hands on her shoulders. Although she hadn't told it to, her body swayed toward him. "I think I'm getting a telepathic message from you, Ashlee," Locke murmured huskily, lowering his head to hers

Ashlee yielded her mouth to him and clung to his strong frame, her eyes tightly shut as heated waves of sensual excitement washed over her. This was crazy, she thought dizzily. She and Locke were hopelessly incompatible, weren't they? Yet when he looked at her in that certain way, when he touched her, all her usually dependable common sense seemed to evaporate. She felt helpless and hot and weak, unable to think at all.

A slow, languorous warmth filled her as Locke molded her to his hard body. Ashlee found herself wishing that they weren't wearing their bulky coats. She wanted to be closer to him, much closer. Her breasts swelled and tightened and she longed to feel his hands upon her.

The kiss went on and on, and Ashlee sank deeper into the warm velvet mists enveloping them. Their tongues met and teased and lured as the kiss deepened in passionate urgency.

"This damn coat," Locke muttered some moments later, pressing her tightly against him.

His voice echoed her own frustration. "I'd like to tear it off you."

"Then I'd freeze." Ashlee managed a shaky little laugh. "Your Yankee winter weather is—"

"—too cold for a little Southern magnolia like you?" Locke teased her, nipping at her lips with a dozen playful little kisses.

Ashlee tried to respond to the lightened mood, but she was aching for the satisfying pressure of his mouth. "Locke," she whispered when she could stand no more of the feather-light, teasing caresses. "Kiss me—hard."

Locke stared down into her soft brown eyes, then groaned her name and took her mouth with a ferocity that made her breath catch in her throat. Hungry ardor flared like wildfire between them. Ashlee lost all sense of time and place as she gave herself up to the thrilling sensations erupting inside her. It was Locke, only Locke who could make her feel this way.

Neither heard the two couples approaching the car parked next to them until the small group was almost upon them. Ashlee and Locke sprang apart like a pair of guilty teenagers, their faces flushed. Ashlee was aghast—to be caught necking in a parking lot! And she had thought Bryce and Lori adolescent! At least they'd had the sense to do their necking in the relative privacy of the car. She and Locke had been on display, for everyone to see.

Locke appeared equally shaken. "Let's go in," he said tightly, wrapping an arm around Ashlee's waist and rushing her toward the door of the restaurant. Neither said a word during that short, tense walk.

The other Aameses and their dates were waiting inside in the fern-filled vestibule. "There you two are!" Alec greeted them jovially, his gaze sweeping over Ashlee's tousled hair and slightly swollen lips. "What took you so long?" He gave Ashlee a knowing wink and she managed a weak smile in return.

She'd never known quite how to react to winking men. She cast a quick glance at Locke. He met her eyes and did not wink. Ashlee felt ridiculously pleased that he hadn't.

"We were—uh—locking up the car." Locke fabricated his answer when Alec asked where they had been for the second time.

"Sure!" teased Alec, winking again. Locke and Ashlee exchanged pained glances.

"Shall we go in to the sushi bar?" Bryce suggested, staring from Ashlee to Locke with a speculative frown.

"Let's go," seconded Garrison Kramer, and the group followed him down the narrow hallway.

When they were all seated at a counter, Ashlee stared with horror at the knife-wielding chef who was slicing thin cuts of raw fish into bowls of rice. She gulped.

"Give the *itamae* your order, Ashlee," Locke said.

"The *itamae* is the chef," Amber explained, and Ashlee was so thrilled that Amber had spoken to her unsolicited, that she beamed. "I'll just have whatever you're having," she said.

When a bowl of rice topped with raw fish was placed in front of her a few minutes later, Ashlee's eyes widened in apprehension. They were actually supposed to eat this? As it was? Eat those little pieces of . . . *raw fish*? She shivered.

"Marvelous!" she heard Cynthia exclaim. "Try the tuna, Alec."

Tuna? Ashlee eyed the concoction in front of her. It looked nothing like the tuna that came out of a can. She glanced at Locke, who was sitting on her left, and at Garrison Kramer on her right. Amber was seated on the other side of Kramer. All were eating and, seemingly, enjoying. Ashlee swallowed hard. As a child she'd flatly refused to touch any type of fish. Only as an adult had she learned to appreciate broiled lobster and deviled crab and fried shrimp. That was as far as her taste for seafood ran, and all of those dishes were *cooked*. But this . . . She couldn't, she simply couldn't.

"Ashlee, you're not eating," Garrison Kramer said, and Ashlee felt all eyes upon her. She was already the outsider in this group, to refuse to eat what they all seemed to like would set her even further apart. Ashlee bravely lifted a piece of fish to her lips and put it into her mouth. It was cold and the squishy consistency nearly made her gag. She kept chewing, trying desperately to pretend that she was actually eating Gran's chicken and dumplings. Or a peanut butter sandwich or pudding or anything but what she actually was eating. Raw fish!

None of her mental tricks worked. Every single one of her senses was revolted by the fish and her stomach joined in the protest. "Excuse me," she murmured breathlessly, and bolted from the counter. She was all right as soon as she reached the rest room. Being removed from the sushi bar and the prospect of eating there seemed to have enacted the cure. Ashlee found a Life Saver in her purse and popped it into her mouth, then washed her hands. She let the warm water run over her wrists for a long time. What was she going to do now? She couldn't face the sushi again, but she could hardly hide out in the women's lounge all night either.

"Ashlee, are you all right?" Lori entered the rest room looking concerned. "We were wondering what happened to you. You've been gone twenty minutes."

It had been Lori, not Amber, who had come to check on her. Ashlee was swamped with gloom. Perhaps Sandy had been right. Maybe she should have talked to Amber herself instead of madly rushing in where even fools fear to tread. She gave Lori a bleak stare.

"Locke says if you don't come out with me, he's

coming in after you," Lori said worriedly. "I think he'll do it, too, Ashlee."

"Thermodynamic physicists don't go charging into the ladies room," Ashlee said dryly, and had to smile at the image evoked

"Let's not risk it," Lori said.

Locke was waiting outside the door, and Lori left the two of them alone. "Are you all right, Ashlee?" he demanded. "You look pale."

"Merely an optical illusion. Actually I'm green."

Locke's eyes narrowed. "I didn't know whether you took off because you weren't feeling well or . . . because of what happened in the parking lot."

"I've never been one to run from a problem, Locke." Ashlee squarely met his enigmatic gaze. "If I were upset by what happened, I wouldn't run and hide." A tiny smile quirked her mouth. "I'd hit you with it right between the eyes."

"Then you aren't well?" He sounded concerned.

"I'm fine as long as I'm away from the sushi bar."

Locke laughed and took her hand in his. "I guess sushi is an acquired taste."

"Not for me." Ashlee shuddered. "Not in this lifetime."

"I think you'll like the next part of the meal much better." Locke lifted her hand to his mouth and brushed his lips across her knuckles in a casually tender gesture that sent a piercing dart of pleasure deep into her womb. "We've moved into one of the dining rooms for our main course."

"Cooked, I hope?"

"Cooked right in front of your eyes on a tableside grill." They entered the dining room and removed their shoes to sit on the floor cushions at a long, low table. Ashlee ordered steak teriyaki, which looked and sounded promising. It was absolutely delicious. But her problems with the food had been solved only to give way to another, more complicated kind of trouble.

Five

Ashlee was sitting between Locke and Alec and directly across from Garrison Kramer. Alec was completely monopolized by Cynthia, thus eliminating him from the general conversation. The same situation existed with Bryce and Lori. It was only natural for Garrison to strike up a conversation with Ashlee, seated across from him, particularly as Amber seemed disinclined to make small talk. Or any talk at all.

Ashlee felt panic rise within her. What could she do? She could hardly snub the man's direct questions, and her answers to those questions revealed a host of common interests. She and Garrison shared the same tastes in music, movies, and, yes, television programs. He had a ready sense of humor and was fun and easy to talk to—and obviously felt the same about her.

Garrison Kramer liked her, Ashlee noted, her stomach churning with anxiety. She was already paranoid from Locke's "come-on" accusations. Was Amber sitting there smoldering with jealousy? Her sister's blank expression gave no clues, and

Ashlee desperately tried to bring Amber into the conversation. She redirected questions to her, she asked her opinions. Amber remained maddeningly unresponsive, replying in shrugs or monosyllables, seemingly bored by it all. Garrison reacted to his date's indifference by concentrating solely on Ashlee.

What was the matter with her sister? Ashlee wondered, baffled by Amber's determined withdrawal. Hadn't Locke said that she'd admired Kramer for months? Why was she treating him like a nonentity? Surely her sister knew that silence and feigned indifference was not the way to win hearts—or friends either, for that matter. And Ashlee was certain that Amber's indifference to Garrison Kramer *was* feigned. It was an intuitive feeling and she'd learned to trust those little flashes of insight. Ashlee redoubled her efforts to discourage Garrison Kramer's interest.

She turned her full attention to Locke. Maybe if Kramer thought she was besotted with Locke Aames, he would give up and turn his charms on Amber. Ashlee moved her cushion as close to Locke's as she dared, taking care to brush his shoulder, his arm, his thigh with hers, often and obviously. She brought him into her conversation with Garrison by using the tactics that had failed on Amber—redirecting every question to Locke, asking his opinions—and added a few more. Ashlee hung on Locke's every word, marveled over any statement he uttered, laughed appreciatively at any humorous remark. She gave him melting smiles and gazed soulfully into his eyes when he spoke. By the time the dessert dishes had been cleared, she was ready to call the operation a success. Garrison seemed to have taken the hint and turned his attention back to Amber.

Ashlee relaxed for a moment and mentally urged her sister on. For Pete's sake, talk to the man, Amber, smile! It was painful for Ashlee to watch.

Amber was so stiff, so terribly serious and reserved. Her face looked ready to crack from the forced, fixed smile. For Ashlee, who made conversation as easily as she breathed, it was a terribly frustrating sight to behold—her sister struggling at something that came so easily to herself. Ashlee began to gnaw at her thumbnail again.

"No nail biting, Ashlee." Locke's amused voice startled her. She'd almost forgotten him, she had been so absorbed in watching Amber. "I remember Mother painting Amber's nails with an evil-smelling liquid to break her of that habit."

"Amber bit her nails?" At last she and her twin had something in common! Ashlee realized that she was really straining for the silver lining by gratefully seizing on that. Perhaps she and Amber could compare notes on nail-biting. It wasn't much of a topic, but at this point it was all she had.

"Ashlee?" Locke's voice, deep and intimate and sexy, instantly captured her attention. She turned to him, and the way he was smiling at her obliterated all thoughts of Amber from her mind. He lifted her hand to his mouth and pressed his lips against her palm. "Let's see if we can distract you from biting that nail." His tongue traced a provocative little pattern on her palm.

A queer shudder coursed through her, and Ashlee was suddenly excruciatingly aware of just how close she was sitting to him. When she'd been concentrating on discouraging Garrison Kramer, she'd been too involved with her part to be fully cognizant of the warmth of Locke's shoulder against hers, of the nearness of his arm to her breast, of the muscular thigh pressed close to her own. Locke began to follow the shape of each one of her fingers with his lips while his eyes caressed her boldly, lingering on her breasts until her nipples budded with heat, focusing on her mouth until her lips parted to draw a shaky, shallow breath.

Locke was responding to her earlier loverlike

behavior by attempting to arouse her. Attempting? Ashlee felt a syrupy warmth course through her lower limbs. He was succeeding. What now? It wasn't going to be easy to explain that she had merely been using him as a prop to help Amber reclaim Garrison Kramer. At this point it wasn't easy to convince herself of it!

Garrison enthusiastically suggested going somewhere for drinks and dancing, and while Amber looked reluctant, Lori and Cynthia eagerly seconded the motion.

"I think Ashlee and I will go home instead," Locke said, and Ashlee was relieved. She did not want to prolong this already-endless evening. "Bryce and Lori can ride with you, Alec," he added, his gaze fixed on Ashlee.

"Won't it be too crowded?" Bryce seemed a bit miffed.

"Of course not!" Garrison boomed heartily. "Amber can sit in the front with Alec and Cynthia and I'll sit in back with Bryce and Lori. There'll be plenty of room."

Ashlee looked quickly at Amber, and for one brief unguarded moment she saw the bleak despair in her sister's brown eyes. Damn Garrison Kramer! How dare he treat her sister this way!

"Let's go, Ashlee," Locke said, his voice husky and close to her ear. As he helped her up, Ashlee saw the hot gleam of desire in his eyes and realized she had been extremely convincing in her role of besotted Locke-admirer. Locke thought she was crazy about him! And his refusal to accompany the others had nothing to do with bringing the evening to an early end. He planned to end it another way, his own way, alone with her. In bed?

"Uh, Locke," Ashlee began tentatively. It was best to be open and honest, to set the record straight right away.

"Yes, Ashlee?" Locke helped her on with her coat, lifting the dark honey-blond curtain of hair with his hand as he leaned down to kiss the nape of her neck. Ashlee's lids fluttered shut for a precarious second. What had she been about to say?

They left the restaurant a few minutes after the others, holding hands. Ashlee caught a glimpse of their reflection in the long glass windows on both sides of the door. Locke towered above her, his large hand firmly clasping her smaller one, and the sight of the two of them together sent shock waves of pleasure through her. They made an extremely attractive couple, she thought with unexpected pride. They looked as if they belonged together.

Ashlee glanced up to find him staring down at her, and their eyes met and held for a long moment. The world around them faded into oblivion, leaving the two of them alone and absorbed only in each other. It was a curious moment of wordless communication charged with sexual tension. Ashlee drew a deep breath and tried to shake off the sensual spell of those intense gray-green eyes. If he could devastate her with just a look . . .

"I enjoyed the dinner. Her voice sounded breathless and high to her own ears. "The steak and the rice and those delicious vegetables. What was the name of that dish?"

Locke's hand encircled the back of her neck, his long fingers beginning a gentle massage. "Oshitashi. Broiled spinach with sesame sauce. I'm glad you enjoyed it."

His touch, his voice were making her weak. Ashlee speeded up her pace, escaping his stroking hand, and hurried to the car, her legs rubbery. Locke Aames was a force to be reckoned with, the first and only man to reduce her to this quivering state. Where was the take-charge Ashlee, the strong one in control of every relationship? Locke had mentioned that she was one step ahead of him. The truth was *he* was in the lead. And Ashlee was alarmed by her own vulnerability. It was definitely time to level with Locke—and resume command of the situation.

Ashlee planned her little speech as Locke caught up with her. "We have to talk," she said, unconsciously imitating Amber's briskly strident tone. First she would tell him that she could not sleep with a man she'd known less than a day. Next she would confess that her ardent behavior this evening had been intended solely to mislead Garrison Kramer. And I'm sorry if I've misled you as well, Locke, she would say apologetically but firmly.

"Say that again," Locke demanded.

"What?"

"The way you said 'we have to talk.' You sounded exactly like Amber."

"I did? 'We have to talk,' " she repeated, and a thrill of recognition flickered through her. "I did sound like her, didn't I?" Somehow it made her feel a little bit closer to her aloof, unapproachable sister.

"Identical twins do have similar-sounding voices, of course." Locke opened the car door for her and Ashlee climbed inside. "But the difference in your regional accents disguised the similarity in your case," he continued as he started the engine. "And of course, the actual tone of voice makes a difference too." He steered the car from the parking lot into the street. "Your voice is usually lilting and pleasant while Amber tries to sound like some oppressive Gestapo type."

"If you dare to suggest that I give her elocution lessons, I'll hit you, Locke Aames."

"You would, too, wouldn't you?" Locke laughed. "I believe you really were the holy terror you claimed to be."

"Well, I haven't yet found you perfect, as you claimed to be." They laughed together, and Ashlee felt a warm sense of companionship, of understanding, between them. What she'd thought to find with Amber, she realized with a little shock.

"Do you know I can hardly believe we met only a few hours ago?" Locke's voice was suddenly husky, and his hand dropped to lightly cover her knee. "I feel I know you so well."

His words jogged Ashlee's memory. She was just going to talk to him about the brevity of their acquaintance and his expectations for tonight. But even as the thought occurred to her, Locke slipped his hand under the hem of her skirt, his fingers skimming along the inside of her thigh.

Locke's hand moved higher and when he touched the bare soft skin above the top of her stockings, Ashlee reeled from the intense pleasure that exploded within her. She closed her eyes and drew a deep breath. An urgent little moan escaped from her throat, and she shivered under the expert caresses of his fingers.

"You're so soft, Ashlee, so warm and desirable," Locke said hoarsely, stroking the silky skin. "Your skin is as smooth as satin." His fingers crept higher and grazed the lacy edge of her panties. "I want to touch you here, to feel *all* your softness and your warmth."

Ashlee was lost in an intoxicating, erotic dream. She kept her eyes closed, and her breathing became rapid and uneven. She languidly shifted her legs in unconscious enticement.

"I want you, Ashlee." Locke's voice, passionate in its intensity, thrilled her. "So very much, sweetheart."

She was moved by the small catch in his voice, by the knowledge that his own urgency made him vulnerable too. Almost of its own volition her hand trailed along his thigh and rested there, just inches from the straining force of his taut masculinity. Locke drew a deep, shuddering breath.

The sharp, furious blare of a car horn jarred them both from their private sensual cocoon to the shock of reality. The traffic light in front of them beamed a bright green. Several other horns joined in the protest and one car pulled past them, illegally on the right, and the driver shouted out the open window, "It's not going to get any greener. Move, you idiot!"

Locke withdrew his hand with a muttered oath and gunned the engine, peeling out with the speed of a 1950's hot-rodder. Ashlee scooted to the opposite end of the seat and huddled against the door.

"I'm completely mortified," she whispered after a few minutes of ghastly, unnerving silence.

"It was my fault," Locke said through tight lips. Ashlee knew that he was equally mortified, but the knowledge offered little consolation. "You have a way of making me feel like a teenage stud." He gave a harsh, self-mocking laugh. "And I was behaving like one too. Ashlee, I'm sorry."

Ashlee sank her teeth into her lower lip so hard that she winced. She was so embarrassed, she wanted to disappear, and Locke's apology somehow made it even worse. "Could we just drop the subject?" She didn't sound like Amber now. Her voice was weak and tremulous and she winced at the sound of it. She didn't even sound like herself. Nor had she been behaving like her normal self.

"Do you mind if I put on some music?" Locke asked in a strained, formal tone. She shook her head and he flipped a cassette into the car's tape player. An instrumental jazz concert filled the air. Ashlee hardly heard it, so involved was she in her mental self-castigation.

She'd done it again! Lost control when Locke had touched her, been reduced to a passionate stranger, unknown to herself. It was almost frightening the way he made her go out of her head like this. It gave him a power over her that no one had ever possessed. And consider the facts! She had only known him for a matter of hours. Worse, when she'd first met him he had been with another woman, Cynthia.

Ashlee remembered the sight of the two of them

sitting side by side on the sofa, Cynthia's knees touching his thigh, Locke's hand just millimeters from her breast. The image sent a searing pang of jealousy scorching through her. How easily and rapidly Locke had shifted his attention from one woman to another! Did that mean he viewed women as interchangeable? It was a thoroughly demoralizing thought and she scowled fiercely.

"What are you thinking?" Locke asked softly, and Ashlee dug her nails into her palm.

"I'm thinking that I badly underestimated you, Locke Aames," she said.

Locke frowned. "What do you mean?"

"When I first met you I thought you were probably a repressed, overly intelligent, scientific stiff. You even confirmed it when you told me that you preferred physics to women. I can't believe I was fooled by the old wolf-in-sheep's-clothing trick. You change women as easily as you change socks, and you're far more dangerous than an obvious flirt like your brother Alec. A woman feels safe with you and then you stagger her with your—your dynamite technique!"

"Dynamite technique?" Locke echoed, sounding tremendously pleased. As well he should, Ashlee thought crossly. "Do you really think so?" he asked.

She glared at him. "I'm not going to write you a testimonial. You know darn well that you—"

"No," Locke interrupted. "You are the first and only woman who has ever considered me more dangerous than Alec. If you were to poll the women I've known, I'm afraid they would concur with your original impression of me—a repressed, overly intelligent, scientific stiff."

"Not Cynthia," Ashlee said, not believing him. No woman, not even an obtuse Yankee female, could fail to appreciate Locke Aames's compelling masculine sensuality.

"Cynthia!" Locke made an exclamation of disgust. "I told you she's a professional husband-hunter. Any man with what she deems the right credentials will do. When Bryce made it clear that he had no intention of marrying, she moved right on down the line to me. I found it rather amusing, to tell you the truth. This afternoon she engineered a 'chance encounter' in the M.I.T. faculty parking lot. I thought such ingenuity should be rewarded and invited her back to the house." He started to laugh. "Enter Ashlee Martin with a plate of banana fritters. End of story. It was perfectly natural for Cynthia to set her sights on Alec, the next available Aames."

"And if I hadn't entered with those banana fritters, would you have taken her to bed?" Ashlee asked coolly. She was not laughing.

"For heaven's sakes, Ashlee, what a question!"

"Under the circumstances, I think it's a very logical question. Since I was responsible for thwarting your little tryst with Cynthia, I'd like to know if I'm supposed to take her place in your bed tonight."

"Of course not!"

"Then you're not rushing me home to bed?" Ashlee asked, her eyes gleaming. "I guess I owe you an apology, Locke. I thought that was just what you had in mind."

"Well, you were wrong, weren't you?" Locke snapped. He turned the volume of the tape higher and the interior of the car reverberated with a saxophone solo. Not one word passed between Ashlee and Locke during the rest of the drive back to Aames.

Upon entering the house, Locke politely offered her a nightcap which Ashlee, in equally polite tones, refused. The stiff little courtesies only heightened the aura of tension between them. Ashlee pasted a smile on her face and said, "I think I'll go up to my room now. Good night."

"Ashlee." His voice stopped her in her tracks. She stood on the bottom step, one hand on the polished wooden bannister, her heart beginning to beat an erratic tattoo. Locke stood a few feet away, his expression somber, his gray-green eyes piercing. "I want you, Ashlee, and you know it." His half smile lacked even a trace of mirth. "It goes without saying that I want to make love to you tonight, and Cynthia hasn't a damn thing to do with it. As you also know, I'm sure. You threw her name out only to—to"—he shrugged—"start an argument? I'm not really sure, but you used her as a defense against me. There was no need to resort to such methods, Ashlee. I want to make love to you, but only if you want it too."

This was the way she'd imagined a brilliant physicist to be—cool and rational, devoid of passion and spontaneity. If he had taken her in his arms and kissed her, if he had swept her up and carried her to his bed, she would have been lost. They would have made love; Ashlee didn't even try to pretend otherwise. But it was easy to remain calm and in control when faced with this emotionless Locke. She had a chance to voice all the reasons why she shouldn't become sexually involved with him—reasons which were instantly obliterated the moment he took her into his arms.

"I've never been the type to jump into bed with a man I've known only a few hours, Locke. And of course there is Amber. I came here to develop a relationship with her, not to—to crawl into bed with her brother." Cool, controlled Amber would never understand being swept away by passion. And standing here with the remote, enigmatic Locke, Ashlee found it difficult to believe herself.

"I don't particularly care what Amber thinks. This is between you and me, Ashlee."

He might have been proposing some new equation for all the passion in his voice. Actually he probably sounded *more* enthusiastic about a new equation, Ashlee decided. That cinched it. "Good night, Locke. Thank you for dinner." She started up the stairs. Locke did not return her perfunctory good night nor make any attempt to stop her from leaving.

The yellow bedroom was chilly. Ashlee doubted that the radiator at full steam could compensate for the cold seeping in through the pre-energy-conscious-age windows. She listened to the wind gusting through the trees and one particularly strong blast actually rattled the windowpane. Ashlee usually slept in comfortably loose silky teddies or slip-style nightgowns, but tonight she withdrew her trusty flannel Lanz, a voluminous red, white, and blue sacklike nightgown she wore only on the occasional below-freezing night at home. But not even the Lanz was proof against these Yankee winter winds. After her sojourn in the arcticlike bathroom, Ashlee added socks and her robe before climbing into bed.

The sheets were positively icy, and Ashlee covered herself with the wool blanket and chenille bedspread and wished for about six more covers. Eventually her teeth stopped chattering and her body heat began to warm the bed. She closed her eyes and a thousand thoughts and images of Amber and Locke spun wildly through her mind. If she were to review all the events and emotions of this day, she would be awake all night!

Ashlee decided to use an old mind trick once suggested to her by Dr. Cameron to promote relaxation. She pictured herself lying under the big willow tree in the field near Gran's house. It was a warm summer day and she could feel the heat of the sun on her face as she listened to the gentle breeze rustle the leaves in the trees. The mountains rose in the foreground; the sky was a deep blue with white puffy clouds. Ashlee heard the summer sounds of crickets and birds, saw the colorful wildflowers in the fields. . . . She relaxed, and the tormenting thoughts receded. She was warm and content in the familiar, peaceful field.

And then she saw something gold. At first she thought it was flowers, but the picture soon crystallized and Ashlee realized that the golden shapes were actually coins. Peculiar coins that she had never seen before. Foreign coins? And they were on a clock. She saw the Roman numerals clearly. It was a very old clock without hands. Ashlee sat up in bed. No, it wasn't a clock, it was some other type of timepiece. A sundial! In a flash of perceptive awareness she knew what the coins must be. They were the ones Locke had mentioned in the car earlier tonight when he was mocking the field of parapsychology. What had he called the coins? Guineas from the time of King George III. Priceless; his inheritance from his uncle; something to pass down to future generations of Aameses.

Ashlee concentrated on the picture before her eyes. It was definitely a sundial; she saw the stone pedestal and base. But the top was marble and inlaid and the coins were beneath it. If the top was removed, the coins would be found in each corresponding position of the Roman numerals. Twelve coins, a dozen gold guineas, just as Locke and Bryce had said.

Excited, Ashlee threw back the covers and hopped out of bed, forgetting the chill in the room along with the coldly formal way she and Locke had parted earlier. It was always thrilling to locate some lost item of value. She remembered the time she'd found Aunt Judy's prized Elvis record, an early single on the Sun label that Aunt Judy feared was lost forever. Ashlee had seen the record, just as she'd seen the coins in her mind, caught between two drawers in an old chest. Aunt Judy had been so happy she had baked Ashlee's favorite Rocky Road cake, loaded with chocolate chips, marshmallows, and nuts.

Ashlee threw open her bedroom door and raced

into the hall, only to collide full-force with a hard muscular wall. Locke. His arms encircled her, absorbing the impact of her weight without even stepping backward. Ashlee, momentarily winded, gulped for breath.

"Ashlee." Locke's voice was husky and thick. His lips brushed the top of her hair, her forehead, and her cheeks. "Darling, were you coming to me?"

Her ability to breathe restored, Ashlee drew back her head to tell him the thrilling news. "Yes, Locke, I know—"

"And I was coming to you, sweetheart." His mouth closed over hers in a hard, hungry kiss. For a moment Ashlee was too stunned to respond. And then she began to kiss him back, her response as wild and fierce as his. The gold guineas were forgotten as Locke scooped her up into his arms. "I couldn't sleep at all, Ashlee. I couldn't stand the way we parted tonight." He carried her into her room, his long legs taking giant strides. "I wanted you so desperately and I was fighting it, fighting you." He laid her down on the bed. "Ashlee, I want you to know that you are not interchangeable with Cynthia or anyone else. Lord, woman, you couldn't be! I've never felt this way about a woman before. . . . It's like being knocked senseless."

"I think you're complimenting me again," Ashlee said as he lay down beside her. She felt wonderfully, insensibly happy. "Although it's sometimes hard to tell."

"I was only kidding myself when I let you go to your room alone tonight, honey." Locke's hands fumbled unsteadily with the belt on her robe. "I need you so, Ashlee. Sweetheart, I have to have you." He rained feverish kisses over her face, then buried his lips in the curve of her neck.

It would be so very easy to give in to him. This impassioned Locke was oddly vulnerable, and Ashlee was touched by his need. She knew she ought to tell him to leave, for all the excellent reasons she had presented downstairs. But she had been cool and calm and rational then and so had Locke. Now he was kissing her hungrily, telling her of his desperate need of her. He was no longer cool and calm and rational, nor was she. A voluptuous surge of emotion swept through her and she held him closer, wanting to assuage this need of his, wanting him with a fierceness and a tenderness she had never before experienced.

"Locke," she murmured as his mouth touched hers. His tongue slipped inside, probing hotly, seeking a deeper, fuller penetration. Ashlee drew a deep, shuddering breath. His hands moved firmly over her body, making the flannel feel as sensuous as silk to her rapidly heating skin. Her nipples were taut and straining against the thick material and his thumbs found them unerringly, brushing over the hard buds with light, rhythmic caresses that made her moan.

Ashlee had no recollection of Locke shedding his robe, but he must have done so for now he was naked. The bare warmth of his body was an added potent stimulant to her already-spinning senses. Her fingers tangled in the soft mat of hair on his chest, and she ran her hands over the muscular breadth of his shoulders, over the smooth hardness of his back. It was intoxicating to touch him like this, to feel him shudder with want and need under her hands. As she was doing under his.

"Yes, touch me, Ashlee," Locke rasped, and the raw need in his voice coupled with the heat of his throbbing male arousal sent Ashlee spinning over the edge. Her fingers wrapped around him and he groaned as if he were in agony, a maddeningly sweet agony. Ashlee was filled with a thrilling sense of feminine power. She could make Locke Aames go as crazily out of control as he could her. Their passion and their power over each other was urgently, desperately, mutual.

"That's enough, Jezebel-Delilah." Locke

removed her hand, making a sound somewhere between a groan and a husky laugh. "I want to make it last all night, Ashlee. I want to make it good for you."

A silvery glow of moonlight filtered in between the slats of the old-style blinds, silhouetting Locke's body. Ashlee's pulses pounded. He was beautiful, so lean and hard and muscular. How could she have not thought him male-centerfold material? In a rush of erotic tenderness Ashlee buried her face in the warmth of his chest, her tongue finding the nipple. Her hands wandered over the curve of his taut buttocks and his body convulsed in a sudden spasm.

"You have an unfair advantage," Locke said, his voice unsteady as he tugged at her nightgown. "Let's take this thing off."

"This isn't what I usually wear to bed," Ashlee apologized, wishing she were wearing her dusky rose teddy.

"I hope not. You look about twelve years old and very demure. I feel like a child-molester."

She laughed and wriggled out of the nightgown. A rush of frigid air swept over her bare skin and she began to shiver. "Locke, I'm freezing!"

"Don't worry, love, I'll keep you warm." Locke nipped at her lobe and his tongue probed the delicate pink shell of her ear.

But the icy blast had effectively broken the spell of passion and Ashlee emerged to face the consequences of her actions. Nothing had changed since she'd stood on the steps and told Locke why she shouldn't sleep with him. She still had known him less than one day; there was still Amber to consider. If Amber were to find her embroiled in a hot affair with her brother, Ashlee felt certain that any chance of winning her twin's respect, friendship, or love would be blown to smithereens. And it was Amber who was the focus of her lifelong dream,

Ashlee reminded herself sternly. Locke had made a late appearance well into the second act.

"Ashlee?" Locke sensed her withdrawal. He covered her body with his own and nibbled at her neck, whispering sexily to her. It was such an obvious attempt to stir her passion—to get this operation back on the right track as it were—that Ashlee stiffened with irritation and newfound resolve.

"You wouldn't." Locke groaned. "Sweetheart, you wouldn't . . . stop now?"

Ashlee gulped. "I know it—uh—must seem unfair of me, Locke, but—"

"Unfair? That's not quite the word I would use to describe what you're doing to me, Ashlee. Try inhuman or indescribably cruel!"

"I'm sorry." Ashlee set her jaw with stubborn determination. "But I—"

"You're sorry?" Locke interrupted harshly. "I could make you really sorry, little girl. I—I could take you, you know, and there would be nothing you could do to stop me."

Ashlee resisted the urge to leap at the challenge. Part of her wanted nothing more than to engage in a fierce physical struggle with Locke in which he would emerge victorious and she could safely surrender to the violent urges pulsing through her. But why bother to play those games? she wondered wearily. It really wouldn't be fair, to herself or to Locke. "I know you could, Locke," she said softly. "But you wouldn't. You told me downstairs that you wanted to make love only if I wanted it too."

"You do! Or you did. Dammit, Ashlee, do you make a practice of this sort of thing?" Locke's passion was rapidly being transformed into an anger that was equally white-hot. "You said earlier, in the den this afternoon, that you were a tease, but I didn't really take you seriously. Until now! You are the—"

"I'm not a tease," Ashlee cut in hotly. "I told you

that I didn't want to—to do this, but you carried me in here and began to make love to me and I—I couldn't stop. I'm weak where you're concerned, Locke, and you're fully aware of the fact. You chose to take advantage of that tonight."

"You are daring to accuse me of seducing you?" Locke was outraged. He fumbled for his robe and pulled it on while Ashlee did the same with her nightgown. It was a horrid, awkward moment. "You literally ran into me in the hall on your way to my room, lady. Or have you conveniently forgotten that little fact?"

"I was coming to tell you something." Ashlee slipped her robe around her and tied the belt with trembling fingers. Locke coughed his disbelief. "I was! I—I know where your Uncle Charlie's gold coins are, Locke."

Even in the moonlit darkness she could read the contempt in his eyes. He backed away from the bed, his lips twisted into a sneer. "Oh, you've been communing with Uncle Charlie after all? I thought seances weren't your specialty."

"I haven't been communing with anyone! And I've never held, or even been to, a seance in my life. I told you that clairvoyance was extra-sensory perception pertaining to objects and I—"

"Just skip it, Ashlee. I've never been less in the mood for a lecture on the occult than at this moment."

"I'm just trying to explain—" her voice failed her as she watched him walk to the door—"why and how I can sometimes locate things that are missing," she managed to finish.

"Save it for Lori. Maybe you can make a guest appearance at her spook-and-magic class."

"The coins are in a sundial," Ashlee called out defiantly as Locke opened the door and stepped into the hall. "The top piece is inlaid and can be removed and the coins are inside, one where each Roman numeral is positioned on the dial."

The door was slammed shut. Infuriated, Ashlee leaped from the bed and flung the door open again. Locke was already halfway down the hall. "Don't you ever slam the door when I'm talking to you!" she yelled furiously. Locke didn't even turn around, but disappeared into one of the rooms. Ashlee resisted the childish urge to run after him and deck him. She was no longer a juvenile spitfire in Martin country. Grown women didn't resort to sucker punches. She hadn't even been tempted to pull one in years.

Ashlee returned to bed, but her emotions were too volatile to be calmed by a tranquil pastoral image. She remained awake, tossing and turning, her body trapped in a quagmire of physical frustration and pure fury. She hated Locke Aames, loathed him, despised him . . . and even as she muttered to herself she knew it wasn't really true. Another part of her reacted quite differently to another part of him. Never had she been so ambivalent about anyone! It was confusing and maddening and totally consuming. She could think of nothing but Locke, not even when she commanded herself to think about Amber and ways to approach her twin.

Ashlee heard footsteps in the hall an hour later and bolted up in bed. If it were Locke, coming to seek her forgiveness . . . Her heart raced and two scenarios played simultaneously in her mind. In one, she accepted his apology and snuggled into his arms; in the other she treated him to a devastating diatribe and sent him from her room.

As it happened, she got to do neither. The steps passed by her room and continued down the hall, and Ashlee heard whispered voices as they passed. Alec and Amber, home from their dates. Ashlee gave her pillow a vicious punch and pulled the covers over her head.

Six

It was a few minutes past nine when Ashlee awakened, her mental alarm clock functioning with admirable precision despite the long periods of sleeplessness during the night. She washed and dressed quickly, eager to leave the chilly confines of her room for a cup of coffee and perhaps a doughnut. That good old caffeine and sugar rush—how she needed it!

While brushing her hair and securing it on the sides with two tortoise-shell barrettes, she looked closely at herself in the mirror and frowned. She was wearing snug turquoise corduroy slacks and her favorite turquoise, white, pink, yellow, and green striped blouse with a canary yellow sweater-vest. It would be too much to hope that Amber approved of her outfit; so far her twin had viewed her clothes as something akin to an eyesore. But as a conciliatory gesture to Amber, Ashlee had dispensed with all makeup. But at seeing herself, she suppressed a groan. What did it matter that she looked like a ghoul? She wasn't here to attract anyone's attention but Amber's.

Ashlee heard voices in the kitchen as she approached it. One of them she instantly recognized as Amber's. Just the way Amber pronounced the pronoun *she* made Ashlee certain that her twin was discussing her. And though Gran always said that eavesdroppers never heard anything good about themselves, and Ashlee agreed wholeheartedly, she nevertheless stood quietly outside the kitchen door to listen.

"You can't really blame it all on her, Amber." That was Alec's voice, slightly chiding. "She is smiley and sparkly and easy to talk to. And you made no attempt to show the man you were at all interested in him. I've seen more animation in a cartoon."

Ashlee winced. If Alec was talking about Amber's behavior with Garrison Kramer the night before, he was painfully accurate, but to tell Amber so bluntly seemed incredibly tactless.

"I did attempt to engage in serious, intelligent conversation." Amber's voice was cold and stiff. With pain and hurt pride? Ashlee longed to comfort her twin. "I see no reason to indulge in that irrelevant and mindless smiley-sparkly nonsense," Amber continued. "It's pointless, a waste of time for all concerned."

"Which is why Garrison Kramer called this morning and asked for Ashlee and not you," Alec retorted. "You can't be so deadly serious all the time, Amber. And there are other topics of conversation besides banking. You need to lighten up."

Ashlee froze. Garrison Kramer had called her? She stifled a gasp of dismay and hoped she'd heard wrong. Locke, sounding cool and indifferent, dashed that hope. "Did Kramer actually call here and ask for Ashlee?"

"Promptly at eight this morning. I guess he thought she followed Aames hours," Alec said. "You know, I do admire Kramer's style. He was totally open, identified himself, and asked to speak to Ashlee Martin. When I told him she wasn't up yet, he said to tell her that he would call her later."

"Personally I think Kramer is an imbecile," Bryce interjected. "Has he forgotten the name of the bank where he works? Dumping Amber to take up with that fruitcake twin of hers is hardly a sound career move on his part."

"Do you think that I want a man whose sole interest in me is my father's bank?" Amber asked tightly. "Locke, do you . . . think that she'll go out with him?"

"Would you mind if she did?" Locke asked quietly.

"I—I would hate it!" Amber said with more emotion than Ashlee had ever heard her express. "Locke, could you keep her away from him? She seems to have taken a liking to you, and if you could pretend to encourage her, to keep her occupied so that she has no time for . . . him, I'd appreciate it, Locke."

"Consider it done," Locke said, and Ashlee thought she was going to die right there in the hall outside the Aames kitchen. The pain was searing and she berated herself for feeling a thing. Why should it matter that Locke was willing to "encourage her" just to keep her away from Garrison Kramer? Garrison Kramer, whom she hadn't the slightest interest in! she protested in a silent scream. If only she could have talked with Amber. They could have cleared the air and reached a mutual understanding. But Amber was determined to avoid her. Their relationship thus far hadn't even approached the superficial.

Ashlee debated the merits of marching into the kitchen, announcing that she had overheard the conversation, and assuring Amber that she had no designs on Garrison Kramer. But would Amber believe her? Probably not. And the wall between them would grow, perhaps to impassable heights.

She couldn't afford to take that chance. But the worst wasn't over yet.

"Say, while we're on the subject of you and Miss Ashlee, how did it go last night, Locke?" Alec said cheerfully, teasing. "We couldn't help but notice how quickly you deserted the group to rush her home to bed."

Ashlee's face flamed; her whole body felt as if it were on fire. Closing her eyes, she waited to be annihilated by Locke's scathing reply.

"We came home and each of us went to our own bedrooms," Locke answered shortly. "Sorry to disappoint you, Alec."

"Oh. Let me guess." Alec laughed. "She talks a great game but she doesn't come across in the final inning. Too bad, brother."

Someone else laughed—was it Locke or Bryce?— and Ashlee realized that she was shaking. With nerves? Anger? Or relief? She hated being the topic of such men's-locker-room talk, but was deeply thankful that Locke hadn't mentioned their bedroom fiasco.

"That girl is a twenty-four-karat kook," Bryce said disparagingly. "Certifiable. And not quite as stupid as she originally seemed. I find myself questioning the timing of her arrival here."

"Oh, Bryce," Locke said. He didn't refute any of his brother's assertions, though, Ashlee noted indignantly.

"Don't you think it's more than a little suspicious that this long-lost twin sister should show up just seven weeks before Amber's twenty-fifth birthday?" Bryce's voice grew louder as he warmed to the subject. "And what is the traditional Aames twenty-fifth birthday celebration? That each of us finally comes into full control of our trust fund! At twenty-five Amber will be in complete control of five million dollars, a fact her colorful little twin is undoubtedly fully aware of."

Ashlee's jaw dropped. Was Bryce Aames accusing her of . . .

"Do you really think Ashlee knows about the trust? And that Amber will be in full control of it on her birthday?" Alec asked doubtfully.

No! Ashlee protested in silent shock.

Bryce snorted. "Of course. But she tipped her hand last night when she started raving about all that paranormal nonsense."

"What?" chorused Alec and Amber.

"Your twin has a passion for the occult," Bryce said. "And I'm sorry to report that she fancies herself a psychic, Amber. So be forewarned. I predict she is planning on using some of this mind-bending voodoo on you to finagle money from your trust fund."

Ashlee leaned against the wall, staggered by the accusation. It took every ounce of willpower she possessed to keep from flying into the kitchen and refuting his ugly speculations.

"You mean she might try to hypnotize me or something?" Amber sounded amused. "Honestly, Bryce, you don't think I could be taken in by threats or black magic or superstitions, do you? I deliberately walk under ladders and encourage black cats to cross my path. I assure you I'm immune to anything out of the twilight zone."

"I wouldn't treat it so lightly," Bryce admonished her. "To be forewarned is to be forearmed, Amber."

Ashlee swallowed around a huge lump that had risen in her throat. Would Bryce's absurd suspicions irrevocably poison Amber against her? First the matter with Garrison Kramer, and now this! How could she ever overcome such overwhelming obstacles and reach her twin? And Locke, he hadn't said a word in her defense. But then, he was angry with her about last night. And perhaps he agreed with Bryce? That notion was almost unbearably painful. To be thought some sort of con artist here to bilk her own twin sister out of money that she hadn't even known existed until this moment . . . For Locke to think that of her . . . A flood of hot tears swam in her eyes.

"Now that I've warned Amber, Locke, I feel I must caution you as well," Bryce droned on with self-righteous pomposity. "Take care around that girl. She may have decided to leave nothing to chance. And she does know about the law of chance; she let that slip in the car, remember? My guess is that she has an eye on snaring a rich husband as a back-up plan, in case her scheme to extort money from Amber fails."

Locke gave a shout of laughter. "You've become a regular misogynist since your divorce, Bryce. I don't think there's a woman alive that you trust."

"I most definitely trust Mother," Bryce replied stiffly.

"Only Mother? What about me?" Amber asked.

"And you, too, of course, Amber. But I do worry about your being taken in by your twin. I can understand the strong pull of genetics and heredity, particularly in one who—" Bryce broke off abruptly.

"Particularly in one who has no other blood ties?" supplied Amber in a flat tone. "You don't think that my loyalty and feelings for this family are as strong as yours because I was adopted and not born into it?"

"Amber, you're as much an Aames as any one of us," Locke said firmly.

"But I'm the only Aames to have an unknown twin arrive on the doorstep," Amber cried bitterly. "That couldn't possibly happen to any of you! You weren't given away by your mother. You've known who you are and who is related to you all your lives."

Ashlee couldn't stand to listen anymore. And as much as she wanted to run upstairs to her room and hide, her stubborn pride precluded any such action. But how should she handle this situation?

Storming into the kitchen and angrily refuting everything she'd overheard would hardly improve her credibility with the doubting Aameses. They might be embarrassed that she'd overheard them, but their attitude toward her would probably remain unchanged.

Ashley weighed her options. She could leave for Chapel Hill right now and give up any chance of ever knowing her sister, simply settling for the knowledge of her name and whereabouts. Or she could stay here and refute their suspicions by her actions, to continue to try to win Amber's love. For Ashlee there really wasn't a choice. She had hoped and dreamed and searched too long to simply call it quits.

She would give herself a week to develop some sort of rapport with Amber. If she failed by the end of that time, she would go home at least knowing that she hadn't given up without a fight. A true Martin. But she would have to proceed with caution. Not another word about her psi ability; perhaps that would lay to rest their suspicions of her alleged charlatanism. And while she would go along with Locke's attempts to "keep her away from Garrison Kramer" she wouldn't make the foolish mistake of believing in Locke's feigned interest in her. She would remember—always— that having been kicked out of her bed the night before, Locke Aames would only be trying to protect Amber from her man-stealing extortionist twin. And naturally Ashlee would avoid Garrison Kramer as one would avoid a carrier of the bubonic plague.

Angrily suppressing an urge to burst into tears, Ashlee pasted a smile on her face and pushed open the kitchen door. The four Aames siblings were seated at the kitchen table. All of them were dressed in sweat suits, and by the looks of them had already indulged in a strenuous morning exercise session.

"Good morning," Ashlee sang out cheerfully, watching their faces. Did they look uneasy, as if worried about what she might have overheard? Or was it merely her imagination, projecting what she already knew? "You're all up bright and early."

"Early?" Bryce snorted. "We've been up since six, jogged our usual five miles, and put in some time at the gym."

"We have a small but very well-equipped gym right here in the house," Alec added with his customary charming smile.

"Now, why doesn't that surprise me?" Ashlee returned his smile. "Where are Sharon and Brian this morning?" She wished they would make an appearance. The children's presence would break this awkward tension surrounding them all.

"They were collected at seven-thirty this morning by their maternal grandparents, the Harcourts," Bryce replied dourly.

A prior arrangement, or a hastily concocted one to remove Sharon and Brian from her pernicious influence? Ashlee wondered sardonically. Her gaze flicked over the food on the plates in front of the Aameses, and her eyes widened. Bryce and Amber were each eating a dish of prunes that they had topped with a dollop of plain yogurt. Alec and Locke were eating some type of cereal—at least she assumed it must be cereal. Actually it bore a closer resemblance to what she and her cousins used to feed their hamsters.

"Sit down, Ashlee, have some breakfast." Locke patted the empty chair next to him. So he was ready to begin to fulfill his promise to Amber, was he? Ashlee wondered. He was even going to pretend to forget the hostilities of last night. If she hadn't overheard his promise to Amber, she might have been stupid enough to believe that his smile was genuine, that he really did want to put last night behind them and begin anew. But Ashlee was on her guard and she indulged in no such wishful thinking.

She sat down and gazed at the prunes and yogurt and the unfamiliar health-food grain. It was not a Martin-type breakfast. "I guess you don't have any Pop-Tarts?" she asked wistfully. "Or doughnuts?"

She felt the collective shudder around the table.

"It's a great mistake to load up on high-sugar carbohydrates the first thing in the morning, Ashlee," Locke explained in a patient, professorial tone. "Or at any time, really. You get that sudden rush of energy from the sugar, but then you crash. You should eat a well-balanced, nourishing breakfast."

"Sometimes I do," Ashlee said, proffering the olive branch in their phony truce. "In fact, some fried eggs and bacon and hash-brown potatoes sound just right. I'll whip up a batch of biscuits too. Anybody care to join me?"

Four pairs of eyes stared at her, mirroring a range of emotions from horror to disapproval to sheer distaste. "A meal like that would send your cholesterol levels clear off the charts." Bryce said, all but shuddering.

"Everything . . . fried . . . and all that butter!" Amber said.

Ashlee gave up. "I guess I'll just have toast," she said, and everyone seemed relieved. It was too much to hope that commercial white bread would be found in the house, but she wasn't averse to whole wheat, and toasted two slices. There was no butter, of course, only some sort of poly-unevery-thing low-cal margarine. There was no jam or jelly either.

"We never have it," Locke said when she requested it. "Jams and jellies are loaded with white sugar. Poison."

Ashlee decided she had better not request that poison to sprinkle over her toast. Sugar bread was an old Martin family favorite, but she feared the Aameses would have a collective cardiac arrest at the sight of it. The coffee was decaffeinated, naturally, and Ashlee settled for tea, which wasn't. One by one the members of the Aames family departed from the table, finally leaving Ashlee and Locke alone in the kitchen.

"What would you like to do today, Ashlee?" Locke asked as she sipped her tea. "Some sightseeing? I think you would like Old Cambridge. We could do the walking tour and have lunch and then I'd show you around Harvard and M.I.T. And, of course, there is all of Boston to see."

"All this in one day?"

"We'll do as much as we can fit in."

Ashlee cast him a wry glance. He certainly believed in following through on his promises. He was obviously prepared to spend the entire day with her, just to keep her from getting Garrison Kramer's phone call. Ashlee wondered if Amber appreciated her adoptive brother's loyalty. "Could Amber come with us?" she asked, guessing the answer even as she voiced the question.

"You can ask her along, of course, but if I know Amber, she intends to spend the whole day studying. Ashlee, about last night . . ."

Yes, how was he going to resolve last night? Ashlee mused. He would have to come up with a plausible reason as to why he was no longer angry with her, why he wanted to spend the day with her. "I'd rather not talk about last night, Locke," Ashlee said truthfully. She didn't want to hear the reason he'd invented to deceive her.

"I want to talk about it, Ashlee. I want to acknowledge it and bring it out in the open. And I want to apologize for the way I behaved."

"Apologize?" He'd caught her off guard with that one. "But I was the one who . . ."

"Ashlee, you had every right to call a halt when you did and I was wrong to slam out of your room like a spoiled brat who's been thwarted for the first time in his life. You told me the reasons for your decision and I should have respected that decision. I *do* respect it, Ashlee."

"In the cold light of morning?" she teased.

"After a couple of cold showers," Locke admitted with a rueful laugh. "Forgive me, Ashlee? Can we put it behind us and make a fresh start?"

Oh, he was good, Ashlee thought. He fairly radiated contrition and sincerity, and had she not overheard his promise to Amber, she would have been completely taken in by him. "I've never been one to hold a grudge," Ashlee said. Two could play this game. "And it was my fault too, Locke. I agree, let's put it behind us."

"That's not to say that I won't try to change your mind." Locke took her hand and carried it to his lips. "I want you, Ashlee. More than I've ever wanted any other woman."

Ashlee made no reply. She didn't doubt that he wanted to take her to bed, but the part about wanting her more than any other woman was overdoing it. She hoped that he wouldn't continue to make such grand proclamations. It depressed her to hear them and to know he was merely playing a role, reciting lines from some script. She carefully withdrew her hand and picked up her teacup. Locke was watching her with a searching, enigmatic expression.

After finishing breakfast Ashlee went to her room to apply her makeup. She'd decided that she couldn't go through the entire day looking washed-out, although it would serve Locke right if she did.

Thinking of Locke, she wondered if she might be judging him too harshly. Maybe he was sincerely interested in her, and Amber's request had merely been fortuitous. But then, remembering him accusing her of being a tease and of coming on to her own sister's date, laughing at her belief in psychic phenomena, she decided Locke's only interest in her was physical. She was certain he was spending the day with her only for Amber's sake—and that hurt. Forcing aside her unhappy thoughts, Ashlee left her room. She stopped at Amber's bedroom and rapped lightly on the door.

"Come in," Amber called. She obviously wasn't expecting her twin, for her voice was welcoming. Ashlee opened the door. Amber was seated at a large oak desk with books and papers strewn around her. Her hair was still wet from being washed, and she was no longer wearing her sweat suit but navy wool slacks and a navy pullover sweater. Both were too large for her.

"Hi." Ashlee smiled. "You look busy."

Amber eyed her warily. "I am." She seemed to shrink into the large upholstered chair. "I have quite a bit of reading to do and a paper to write."

"For your business courses?" Ashlee wanted to prolong the conversation for as long as possible. She and her sister were alone at last. If only they could make some breakthrough, to communicate somehow, some way . . .

"Yes, for my business courses," Amber replied pointedly, turning her attention back to her books.

Ashlee took a deep breath. "Do you feel like taking a break? Locke has offered to take me sightseeing. I wondered if you'd like to come along?"

"Oh, I can't," Amber said quickly. "I have so much work to do today. I couldn't possibly come with you."

What was Gran's pet phrase? The one she continually drummed into her impetuous grandchildren? Oh, yes, "patience and perseverance." She would try another overture, this one slightly different. "Amber, I'll be going back to North Carolina next weekend, but I hope before I leave we'll have a chance to spend some time together." Ashlee tried to sound nonchalant, but her stomach was churning. Suppose Amber's answer was an unqualified no?

But Amber appeared positively delighted with the news of her twin's definite departure date, so much so that she actually smiled and looked at Ashlee. "Perhaps we can have dinner together some night this week. I almost always work late though. It might not be until after seven."

"That would be fine," Ashlee said eagerly. "Any night, any time." She fairly floated down the stairs. The brief exchange with her twin hadn't been much, but it was at least a start. And now they had definite dinner plans. Well, indefinite definite dinner plans.

She met Locke in the vestibule. He, too, had showered and changed clothes. He wore tan corduroy slacks, a burgundy V-neck sweater, and a white Oxford-cloth shirt. He was compellingly, strikingly masculine and Ashlee felt the force of his attraction like a magnetic pull—an attraction she had to resist.

"You look lovely, Ashlee." Locke smiled at her as she retrieved her coat from the hall closet.

He would have said that if she looked like the bride of Dracula, Ashlee told herself. It was all part of the act. But she had a role to play too. "Smiley and sparkly" Alec had described her. She would play her part to the hilt. Ashlee flashed what she hoped was a suitably smiley-sparkly grin. "Thank you, Locke. You look rather devastating yourself."

"Uh, thanks." Locke looked both pleased and uncertain, as if not quite sure how to respond. He fiddled with his collar and brushed an imaginary speck of lint from his sweater.

"I love the color of your sweater." Ashlee moved closer, her gaze admiring. It was true, she did love burgundy and often teamed it with shades of pink. She looked at Locke's white shirt and decided that a similarly styled pink shirt would really liven up his outfit.

"Amber gave me this sweater for Christmas,"

Locke confessed. "I was afraid it was a bit too bright for me. I usually stick to navy or brown."

Ugh, Ashlee thought. "It's not a bit too bright, Locke," she said earnestly. "It's a wonderful shade for you. And I can just picture you in kelly green or robin's egg blue. They would really bring out the beautiful color of your eyes."

"Oh—uh—er—thanks." Locke seemed totally discomfitted.

Ashlee watched him self-consciously adjust the cuffs of his shirt and tug at his sweater while seemingly studying the old rug on the floor. Why, he was embarrassed! Because she had complimented him on the color of his sweater? "You're blushing," she said with astonishment.

"I guess I am." He gave a self-deprecatory laugh. "I'm not used to receiving lavish compliments on my appearance, or discussing what colors would bring out my beautiful eyes. It's a definite first for me."

"A first?" Ashlee stared at him. She had spent a lifetime listening to her grandmother and aunts telling the male Martins how very good-looking they were in certain colors and styles, and had naturally followed suit. Men liked to be noticed and complimented on their attire, just as women did. How could Yankee women not know that? A thought struck her. "I suppose you've always been complimented on your academic brilliance and scientific genius," she guessed, and Locke nodded uncomfortably.

"Yankees are blinded by brains, I suppose. Show them a high IQ and they immediately lose sight of the hunk containing it."

"Hunk?" Locke laughed. "You're laying it on a bit thick, peach blossom. I am not now, nor ever will be, remotely considered a hunk."

"You don't know how appealing you really are, Locke Aames," Ashlee said thoughtfully. "You thought Cynthia made a play for you simply because you were the next available Aames brother, you think that women consider you a scientific stiff and only admire you for your brains. And you're wrong . . . so very wrong."

Locke stared at her for a long moment, bemused. Then he shook his head as if to shake off the effect of her words. "I'm beginning to see how clichés develop from actual truths. You Southern honeys really do have a way of making a man feel ten feet tall."

"And you Yankee men are simply starved for some of our sweetening," Ashlee teased. Then she thought of Garrison Kramer calling her that morning and Amber feeling rejected and desperate, and her smile faded. Her own twin sister saw her as some kind of man-eater, to be diverted and distracted by the attentions of yet another man. And Locke obviously shared Amber's views.

He was watching her. He saw the playful smile fade, saw the pain flicker in her deep brown eyes. "Ashlee?" He reached out to touch her cheek with his fingertips. "What is it? You suddenly looked so sad."

Why shouldn't she look sad? Ashlee thought. Her twin sister hated her and Locke was only pretending to like her because he thought she was cruel enough to steal Amber's boyfriend unless she was showered with male attention. Sad? She should be bordering on major depression. She was, Ashlee realized, perilously close to feeling very sorry for herself. And self-pity was not a Martin trait. She forced a smile and said brightly, "Why should I be sad? I'm spending the whole day with the most handsome, charming thermodynamic Yankee physicist I've ever met. Also, the *only* one I've ever met."

It was Locke's cue to laugh with her and move on to another topic, something suitably light and impersonal. But Locke missed his cue. He continued to stare down at her, and his hand cradled her cheek gently. "Ashlee, try not to let Amber's lack of response hurt you. I know it must, of course, but keep in mind that Amber's unhappiness has nothing to do with you. She was . . . troubled . . . long before you arrived on the scene."

"Maybe." Ashlee shrugged. "But I've hardly been a ray of sunshine in her life." Whatever had troubled Amber before had been compounded by the fear that her twin was after her boyfriend. Poor Amber. Ashlee longed to reassure her, to try to instill the self-confidence she instinctively knew her sister lacked. "I want Amber to like me, Locke. I want to regain all those lost years we've been apart."

"I know, Ashlee." The warm sympathy in his eyes had a most alarming effect on her. She wanted to fling herself into his arms and be comforted by him. She wanted him to hold her and soothe her until the hurt was gone. Ashlee buttoned her coat with trembling fingers. She wanted to be in his arms and experience the passion they had shared the night before . . . to its complete and rapturous climax. The silent admission unnerved her.

"Ashlee, I want you to know that I'm on your side in all of this," Locke said quietly. "I think it was incredibly callous of the adoption agency to split up a set of identical twins, and I'd like to see you and Amber become sisters in the truest sense of the word."

His words warmed her; perhaps he really meant them too. But she must not forget that he was also helping to keep her and Amber apart. By agreeing to keep her away from the Aames house, he had tacitly admitted that she was a threat to her sister. But perhaps he didn't realize this?

She looked up at him and was startled to find him staring at her intensely, as if trying somehow to read her mind. What was *he* thinking? Ashlee wished she had scored higher in telepathy, but her talents in that area fell woefully behind those in clairvoyance and precognition.

"Shall we go?" Locke extended his hand to her, and she hesitated for only a half second before slipping her fingers around his.

"Yes, let's." She smiled up at him. After all, what was the point in hanging around the house brooding? Amber was busy, and it would be easier for all concerned if she were not in when Garrison Kramer called again. And then there was that other reason, perhaps the main reason why she was going with Locke. Because she wanted to very much.

Seven

Harvard Square, in the heart of Old Cambridge, displayed a striking fusion of the old and the new, exhibiting both European and American influences. Traditional department stores were interspersed with high-fashion boutiques and a plethora of bookstores. Sidewalk cafés and hamburger stands and ice cream parlors shared the same blocks as luxurious restaurants. Locke hustled Ashlee along the Old Cambridge walking tour, which included Cambridge Common, Christ Church, and the Longfellow House. It would have been picturesque and delightful on a balmy spring or summer day, but in the middle of January with the icy winds never ceasing, Ashlee was more than ready to retreat indoors when Locke suggested lunch at a local restaurant called T. T. the Bear's.

They were seated at a table for two and Ashlee pried open the menu with her frozen fingers. Her thin knit gloves had been no match for the bitter cold; she coveted the impenetrable ski gloves that Locke wore. And she needed a hat. She was convinced that last blast of wind had gone directly through her ears and had iced her brain.

"I'll take you to Harvard and M.I.T. after lunch," Locke said. He seemed utterly impervious to the cold. He had been indefatigably cheerful, the quintessential tour guide. "Meanwhile, *The Boston Globe* says this place has the best cheeseburgers in the whole Boston area."

"That's what I'll have then." Ashlee flexed her fingers gingerly. They still seemed capable of motion. Perhaps feeling would return when they thawed. "What are you going to have, Locke?" She fully expected him to order raw fish or raw meat and was determined to appear blasé about it.

Locke grinned as if he knew just what she was thinking. "I think I'll have a cheeseburger too."

"What about your cholesterol level?"

"It's always been inspiringly low." He reached across the table and took her hand. "Good Lord, your fingers are like icicles!"

"My ears are one step beyond icicles. Dry ice, maybe?"

"Honey, if you were cold, why didn't you tell me?" Locke was instantly all sympathy and concern.

He was acting, Ashlee reminded herself. Only acting. "Oh, I'm too good a sport to bow out because of the weather," she said flippantly. "We Martins are made of stronger stuff."

"Well, we're getting you a hat and some decent gloves," Locke announced. "Unless you'd rather call it a day and go back to the house? If you're too cold and have had enough, we could finish our tour some other day."

One might really believe he was concerned about her, Ashlee thought, staring at his hand covering hers. Offering to take her back to the house was certainly a convincing, masterful touch. He was supposed to be keeping her occupied and out of telephone reach. But then, he probably guessed that she would refuse to go back. Which she did. "Oh, no, I'm looking forward to seeing Harvard and M.I.T." She smiled at him. "I'm having a wonderful time, Locke." It wasn't a line from the script she had fashioned for herself. The cold notwithstanding, she was enjoying every minute of her day.

"I'm glad, Ashlee. So am I." Locke held both her hands in his, rubbing warmth into them. "It's been fun showing you the sights that I've come to take for granted. It's like seeing them again for the first time, through your eyes." His fingers intertwined with hers. "I can't remember a day I've enjoyed more."

His eyes met and held hers. Ashlee felt a dart of pure pleasure shoot through her. Steady, girl, she cautioned herself. If she weren't careful, she would find herself believing him simply because she wanted to so very much.

After lunch they went into a ski shop, where Ashlee found a pair of insulated gloves, a banana-yellow wool cap, and a matching scarf. Locke had already paid the bill before she had time to open her purse and reach for her wallet.

"I insist on reimbursing you," Ashlee said as they left the shop.

"Don't be ridiculous. It was my pleasure."

"Locke, you're very generous, but I can't let you buy me these things. I—"

"Why not?" Locke interrupted. "Is there some Southern taboo on accepting outer apparel? We Yankees believe that gifts of lingerie are to be given only by intimates, but a wool cap? And ski gloves? They certainly seem devoid of any sexual connotation, at least to me."

"Of course there's no Southern taboo." Ashlee laughed in spite of herself. "But these things were expensive, Locke, and there is no reason for you to spend your money on me."

"Suppose I want to spend my money on you?"

If brother Bryce were to hear him now, he would

undoubtedly accuse her of some type of invidious mind control, Ashlee thought grimly. "I don't *want* you to spend your money on me, I like to pay my own way. You've already paid for my dinner last night and lunch today. That's enough, Locke."

"All right." Locke flashed her a sudden grin. "I'll let you pay for our dinner tonight."

"Fine," Ashlee agreed, and Locke instantly recanted. "I was only kidding, honey. I don't want you spending your money on me."

"That's my line. And I insist, Locke."

"Ashlee!" He pronounced her name as two sharp syllables.

"Lo-o-cke!" She drawled his into three sing-song ones.

He sighed with exasperation. "Don't be stubborn, Ashlee. Save your money. If you run out of cash—"

"Then I'll use my American Express card," she cut in.

"*You* have an American Express card?"

"I never leave home without it."

He looked so nonplussed that Ashlee felt obligated to explain. She told him about her shop, Creativity, and the expanding popularity of her handmade dolls. "I applied for and received my American Express card two years ago, when the shop finally turned a profit," she added.

"You're a businesswoman!" Locke exclaimed with apparent delight. "I'm going to be wined and dined by a Carolina doll entrepreneur."

"So you've decided to let me buy you dinner after all?" She paused, frowning. "Wait a minute! Since when are we having dinner together tonight anyway? I thought this was only an afternoon excursion."

"Which is going to last late into the evening," Locke said firmly. "I don't care which one of us pays for dinner, Ashlee, but I want you to have it with me. I thought we could drive into Boston after we tour the universities and choose a restaurant there."

"Without returning to Aames?" Ashlee pulled the bright wool scarf over her nose and mouth, leaving only her eyes exposed to the cold. Locke was fulfilling his promise to Amber with incredible thoroughness. How many of Kramer's phone calls would she miss today? Locke obviously intended her to miss them all.

"I really don't see any reason to return to Aames before heading into Boston."

They had reached the small parking lot where the car was parked. "I'm sure you don't," Ashlee replied sweetly. "In fact, I bet you can come up with several excellent reasons why we shouldn't go back."

"Well, we'd be backtracking for one. It would take us twice as long if we were to—"

"Never mind, you don't have to list them," she interrupted. "Believe me, I get the picture."

"Do you?" Locke draped his arm around her shoulders and pulled her against his bulky gray down jacket. A stinging gust of wind swirled around them and Ashlee buried her face in the soft thickness of his coat. Locke's other arm encircled her, holding her tightly.

"Do you know how much I wanted to have you to myself today, Ashlee? Just you and I, away from the house, and even away from Amber."

"And especially away from the telephone," Ashlee muttered into his coat.

"Hmm? I didn't hear what you said, honey."

Ashlee pulled back slightly and looked up at him. The glow in his gray-green eyes confused her. Gran had always maintained that the eyes were the mirror of a person's soul, that one couldn't really lie with his eyes. But Locke appeared to be doing a world-class job of it. His eyes radiated admiration and desire, not deceit. Where was her much-heralded perception now that she really needed it?

Ashlee knew the answer to that one; it had been proven in various tests. Whenever she was very emotional or tense or tired, the ESP messages were somehow blocked before reaching the threshold of consciousness.

A spark of heat suddenly flashed through her. Ashlee heard her heart begin to thud heavily as a throbbing ache pulsed within her. She stared dumbly at Locke's sensual mouth as his head descended toward her, and a wild series of emotions crashed and collided inside her. It was happening again—the heady loss of control and the passionate urgency she felt every time she was in Locke's arms.

Locke touched his nose to her scarf-covered one, his eyes alight with warmth and humor. "I want to kiss you, but you're as inaccessible as a Moslem woman in a chador. How do those Arab sheikhs manage?"

The urge to touch him was irresistible. "Like this." Ashlee jerked the scarf away and lightly brushed her mouth against his. It was meant to be a quick playful gesture, but Locke clamped his hand around the back of her neck, holding her fast, and opening his mouth over hers. Ashlee's eyelids fluttered shut and her lips parted on impact, welcoming his tongue into the moist softness of her mouth. She responded uninhibitedly, arching her body against his hard masculine frame. A tide of passion stormed through her, and she was achingly aware of her need to be closer to him, to absorb him into her very being.

Ashlee heard the adolescent male chortles and admiring, encouraging chant of "Hey, Dr. Aames! Go for it!" before Locke did. She twisted out of his arms and whirled around to see five college-aged students in jeans and parkas disappear around the corner. Their laughter seemed to echo in the sensual silence that had enshrouded Locke and Ashlee.

"Some of your students?" she managed to say in an unsteady voice.

Locke appeared to be in a daze. He stared blindly ahead for a moment, then reached for Ashlee.

"We seem to be making a habit of this." Ashlee said, heading for the car, keeping just out of his grasp. "Necking in parking lots, that is." She reached the car and stood beside the door on the passenger side, waiting for Locke to open it. "I wonder who those kids were?" she murmured, blushing at the abandoned image she and Locke had presented.

"Those kids!" Locke exclaimed, emerging from his trance. "They have to be undergraduates, sophomores no doubt, and in the only undergraduate course I teach. I *hate* teaching kids that age! They are unmotivated and irresponsible and—"

"—roam the streets in packs, catching their exalted professor indulging in most unphysicistlike behavior," Ashlee supplied impishly. Her initial embarrassment had faded, and she found the situation rather amusing, particularly Locke's indignant reaction.

"I only consented to teach the one undergraduate course for the prestige of the physics department," Locke growled. "I should have refused."

"I'm sure the university is extremely grateful." Ashlee tried and failed to suppress a grin. Poor Locke, he looked so disgruntled. He had obviously never been caught out of his role as professor by his students, and he just as obviously didn't care for the lapse.

Ashlee buckled herself in the middle seat belt, right beside the driver, and watched Locke fumble with his keys. Her brown eyes sparkling with mischief, she removed her gloves and laid one hand on his thigh. Locke dropped the keys, then bumped his head on the steering wheel as he attempted to retrieve them. He muttered a fierce oath.

"Poor baby, you really are shook up, aren't you?"

Ashlee choked back a gurgle of laughter. "Don't worry, I'm sure your reputation as an eminent and brilliant physicist will survive intact."

"Well, I do have a certain image to maintain," Locke began, then sighed. "Oh, hell, it's not that! It's just that when I'm with you I seem to behave completely out of character. I simply don't understand it! I didn't go around necking on the streets of Cambridge when *I* was an undergraduate. And now here I am . . . here you are . . . here we are . . ." He scowled. "And now I'm lapsing into incoherence. Another first!"

Ashlee was secretly delighted. Locke wasn't playing a role now. Whatever his intentions when he'd proposed this outing, she knew beyond question that he wasn't thinking of Amber's request or Garrison Kramer's phone call or keeping her away from the Aames house at this moment. "I'm sorry, Locke," she said softly, giving him a melting smile, her eyes shining with a warm invitation.

Locke stared down at her, seemingly mesmerized. He was going to kiss her; he wanted to kiss her badly. Ashlee read the hunger and desire in his stormy gray-green eyes. And, oh, how she wanted to feel and taste his mouth upon hers.

But this time Locke resisted temptation. He inserted the key in the ignition and fiercely gunned the engine. The Oldsmobile lurched forward and then stalled. Cursing, Locke restarted the car and pulled out of the lot.

"That's Harvard," he muttered as they whizzed past a complex of impressive structures.

"Interesting," Ashlee said, nodding as the last building receded from sight. "Definitely a highlight of my trip north. You Yankees really know how to conduct a tour."

"Oh." Locke was totally disconcerted. "Er—I forgot to stop. You . . . um . . . really didn't get to see much, did you?"

"A definite understatement there."

"We'll go back," Locke said at once. "I meant to stop. I don't know why I didn't. I'd certainly planned to."

Ashlee tried not to, but she started to laugh anyway. She'd never seen anyone so thoroughly flustered. It was rather exhilarating to have that kind of an effect on a man. No, not just any man, Ashlee mentally corrected herself. It was exhilarating to have such an effect on Locke Aames. "Never mind, I'll see it some other time," she said. "I'd much rather see your M.I.T. first anyway. Now, why don't you put on one of your tapes and just relax," she added soothingly.

"Do you like the sax?" Locke asked a few minutes later as a lively saxophone duet played along with a jazz piano.

"I'd never really thought about it. I guess so."

"I play the saxophone. Strictly as a hobby now, although I was once considered quite a good player," he added with a note of pride.

"Would an Aames be anything less?" Ashlee said, smiling. "You mentioned that Amber played the flute. Does everyone in your family play an instrument?"

"Oh, yes. Mother plays the violin, Bryce the clarinet, and Alec the trumpet. And although we all took piano lessons, my father puts all of us to shame on it."

"A one-family band. Do you ever all play together?"

"We used to play for the occasional church or charity event, but Alec's wife put a stop to it. She resented the practice time away from her. Bryce's wife, Nancy, didn't like it much either." He shrugged. "You know how possessive women can be."

Ashlee shook her head. "No, I don't. Why couldn't they have found something to entertain themselves with while all of you were practicing?"

"That's what you would do," Locke said thoughtfully. "You aren't the type to sit around and whine and feel neglected." He smiled. "I think you'd be out finding us bookings."

"We Martins are very enterprising," Ashlee agreed, visualizing the scene and smiling.

"Do you play anything, Ashlee?"

"Only the jukebox." Her own musical upbringing contrasted sharply to the Aames family's tastes. There was Gran with her radio playing country music eighteen hours a day, Aunt Judy's cherished collection of Elvis records, and her own and the cousins' devotion to rock. Ashlee's thoughts returned to Amber. The musical differences merely touched on the other, more serious disparaties between her and her sister. She and Amber might just as well have been raised on different planets!

Locke drove on, the jazz instrumental filling the silence. "This is Central Square, the main shopping district of Cambridgeport," he remarked as they drove along a shop-lined avenue.

Locke was visibly proud of the M.I.T. campus and showed Ashlee around with obvious pleasure. He'd earned both his undergraduate and graduate degrees here, as well as his doctorate, he explained. Now he was a tenured professor and research scientist, a fulfillment of his career goal. Ashlee enjoyed the tour and his enthusiasm. She was particularly impressed with the Kresge Auditorium and the Interdenominational Chapel and told him so.

"Both buildings were designed by Eero Saarinen," Locke said proudly.

The man's name was not exactly a household word in Shade Gap, but Ashlee figured he must be an architect. "He's very talented, isn't he?" she said.

"I agree. One of the most innovative." Locke launched into an enthusiastic account of various styles and fads in the field of architecture. Not bad, Ashlee congratulated herself. Locke actually thought they were having a discussion on architecture, a subject of which she knew nothing. Her contribution consisted of nodding occasionally. But she liked to listen to him, to look at him. Locke Aames was the most fascinating, appealing man she had ever met. The mental picture she'd had of herself in the wedding dress with Locke as her groom flashed briefly to mind, as well as the intuitive flash that she would marry him. Was it merely wishful thinking? Or a true precognitive vision? The thought of marrying Locke no longer upset her. It was what she wanted, Ashlee realized with a jolt. Though she'd only met him twenty-four hours ago, she knew. She was in love with him and wanted to be his wife. If her mind picture was correct, she would be. But how to make it come true? She was dealing with a man who put physics before women, who was wary of the institution of marriage because of his brothers' failures. How could she bring him around to realizing how very happy she could make him? Ashlee began to gnaw on her thumbnail as a spiral of anxiety uncoiled within her. She'd come to Aames to show Amber how happy they could be together, and she certainly hadn't had much success in that area. What if she were equally unsuccessful with Locke?

Locke continued the tour, showing her his classroom and his office, and they talked and laughed together so naturally that Ashlee felt the tension within her begin to dissipate. She would somehow make him see how good they could be together, she reassured herself with the return of her usual optimism.

They were strolling along a corridor toward Locke's laboratory when another picture suddenly imposed itself in front of her eyes. Inside an elevator were two young men. One of them seemed to be in a state of panic; his face was very pale and his eyes were round with fear. The other was frantically punching the buttons on the panel to no avail.

The elevator was stuck with the two men trapped in it.

"Locke, is there an elevator in this building?" Ashlee asked, breaking into his explanation on research grants. He stared at her, slightly bemused by the non sequitur. "Yes, there is, in another wing."

"May I see it?"

He gave her an odd look. "You want to see the elevator?"

She nodded.

"Do you mind if I ask why?"

Ashlee swallowed. "I think there are two men trapped in it."

"What?"

"Locke, there's no point in giving you an explanation that you're never going to believe anyway. Just take me to the elevator, please."

"Ashlee, if this has something to do with that clairvoyant nonsense . . ."

"Never mind, I'll find it myself."

He followed her to the elevator, alternating between complaints and jokes about the occult. Ashlee hit the call button and the elevator arrived within seconds, its doors snapping open. No one was inside. She drew a deep breath and once more the picture danced before her eyes. The two young men, trapped in the elevator. The scared one was pounding on the doors, screaming. "It isn't this elevator," she said flatly.

"Not this elevator," Locke repeated, his expression sardonic. "Now, what does that mean? That somewhere in the world someone is trapped in an elevator? Or will be? Or once was? A very imprecise science, this ESP of yours."

"Yes, it is. Quite different from your thermodynamic physics and its irrefutable laws. I'll try another building."

"Ashlee, for crying out loud! Do you have any idea how many buildings there are on this campus? And almost all of them have elevators. How do you know this particular elevator that you're— uh—seeing is around here anyway?"

He wasn't going to like it, but Ashlee took a deep breath and told him anyway. "Both the guys in the elevator are wearing M.I.T. jackets. That's why I think it's a building on campus."

"Oh, I see. These visions of yours come complete with details, right down to what the characters are wearing. Very inventive."

"Locke, I know this must seem very strange to you, but—"

"Strange?" he echoed. "Strange? Why do you say that, Ashlee? This isn't the first time you've pulled this little number on me, after all. This is no stranger than seeing police cars lurking in bushes or Uncle Charlie's golden guineas hidden in a sundial. I shouldn't be at all surprised that you see two men—wearing M.I.T. jackets, naturally—caught in an elevator."

Ashlee's big brown eyes pleaded with him. "Locke, Dr. Cameron says that psi ability is simply a spontaneous, natural gift that some people have and others don't. Like—like a sense of humor."

"Dr. Cameron didn't give you the full story, Ashlee. All these gifts are actually bestowed by fairies at the time of a baby's birth. The nurses in newborn nurseries across the land are continually colliding with these fey creatures who fly around gifting the babies with beauty or genius or humor. Or psi ability, of course."

"Ha-ha." Ashlee scowled. "The physicist is also a comedian."

"But you haven't heard about the bad fairies yet, Ashlee. How do you think people get mean or ugly or stupid?"

"I've heard enough, thank you." Ashlee headed for the door of the building. He couldn't have made his feelings plainer. He put clairvoyance and parapsychology and Dr. Cameron in the same category as fairy tales. She felt totally disheartened.

"Ashlee." Locke caught up with her and grabbed her arm. "This is ridiculous! I'm not going to let you run from building to building checking elevators simply because you have an overactive imagination."

"You're not going to let me?" Ashlee jerked her arm away from him. That did it! "Correction, honey. You're not going to stop me."

"Ashlee, I absolutely refuse to chase after you while—"

"You don't have to come with me. But I'm going to search every building on this campus until I find that elevator. I can't leave those poor guys stranded without at least trying to help. It's Sunday, Locke. If I don't find them, they might have to spend the night there. And I'm fairly certain that one of them is claustrophobic."

"Hey, that's a neat, dramatic touch! But why don't you make one of the victims a pregnant woman in labor instead? That beats claustrophobia for sheer high drama."

Ashlee withheld comment with no little effort. She found herself making excuses for him. Locke didn't believe in the force that allowed her to see what she had seen. Naturally she would seem totally demented to him. An attention-seeking bizarro. Her stomach churned and she cast a quick glance over her shoulder. He was following her to the tall classroom building on the right, although he was carefully keeping his distance. His mouth was twisted into a grim line and he looked angry. Ashlee had a momentary urge to stop and pretend it was all a joke. To say "April Fool" or something and make him laugh. She didn't want Locke angry with her; she wanted him to love her. A rather bleak prospect at this point, Ashlee acknowledged glumly. If he couldn't accept her as she was . . .

The young man in the elevator was crying now and his plight moved Ashlee to increase her efforts. She couldn't simply abandon him. He and his friend were stuck in an elevator somewhere on this campus and she had to find them.

She heard the noises upon entering the sixth building of her search. Ashlee raced to the elevator and pressed the call button. Nothing. Shouts for help arose from the elevator shaft.

"I'll get help," she called back, and was answered with a cry of relieved thanks. Locke leaned against the wall, staring at her, dumbfounded.

"I'm not sure whom to call," Ashlee said coolly. "Maintenance or security?"

"Both, I think," Locke replied at last, staring at her as if he'd never seen her before. "I'll—make the calls."

Twenty minutes later the two students were free. They were M.I.T. seniors, they explained, and had come into the building to look for a missing notebook early that morning. They had been stuck between floors in the elevator for hours and one of them suffered from claustrophobia. He'd been leery of getting into the elevator in the first place and was still shaking from the anxiety-filled ordeal. The campus security officer agreed to drive the students back to their dorm, and the maintainence crew set to work repairing the elevator. Locke, who had not spoken a word since summoning help, simply stared at Ashlee again.

"I guess we'd better be leaving," she said quietly, and he followed her from the building.

"You didn't tell Security how you happened to know the boys were stuck in there," Locke said as they walked along the deserted sidewalk. "You told them you were passing by and heard shouts."

"I wanted to protect your reputation," she replied dryly. "After all, you do have a certain image to maintain, and it simply wouldn't do for a renowned physicist to be found in the company of a psychic."

"That's absurd!" Locke snapped, and Ashlee wondered which part of her statement he was refuting. She decided a change in subject was definitely in order. "Will you take me to see your lab now? I'd really like that."

"After this little adventure you'll find it boring," he said tightly.

Ashlee stared at him for a long moment. "If you say so," she said at last. Jamming her hands into her coat pockets, she walked away from him, fighting the gloom welling up inside her. It was hopeless; Locke would never accept her. They might have been able to overcome the tremendous differences in their backgrounds, tastes, and interests, but her clairvoyance was the final straw. Locke's logical, scientific mind could not believe in the unexplainable. In his field, proof was truth and without adequate proof . . .

Ashlee's thoughts flitted to Amber, her reason for coming here, and she ruefully admitted the truth to herself. At this moment it was Locke's acceptance and Locke's love that she wanted to win. Her twin sister had been relegated to second place.

"Ashlee." Locke came up behind her and took her arm, turning her around to face him. "Ashlee, do you know what the science of physics comprises?"

Ashlee was baffled. What an odd time for him to quiz her about physics of all things! "No," she replied. "I guess I really don't."

"Physics is based upon the understanding that nature can be reduced to a few comprehensive principles, and physicists seek those central ideas by the use of mathematical and logical tools. That is an oversimplified definition, of course, but . . . Do you understand what I'm trying to say?"

He had avoided mentioning the elevator incident entirely, Ashlee noted wryly. "I think I do, Locke.

And what happened today didn't fit into those comprehensive principles. There is no tangible proof or explanation."

"Ashlee, I won't even pretend to understand why or how you . . ."

"Join the club, Locke. No one understands, least of all me. But to deny that ESP exists doesn't annihilate it."

"ESP doesn't exist! Much of what passes for the so-called ESP is actually the result of very keen observation that takes place so rapidly it's almost unconscious. And some people have a special talent for memorizing and putting together miscellaneous facts very quickly. It's these factors—along with coincidence—that explain the ESP phenomenon. Those incidents that aren't the result of chicanery and deft magicians, that is."

Ashlee had never been one to proselytize. Although she found Locke's explanations more difficult to believe than the actual existence of a sixth nonsensory sense, she didn't challenge him. She'd met other people who absolutely refused to recognize the existence of psi and she had never tried to argue them out of their beliefs. Locke was entitled to his own opinion, however contrary to hers. "Okay," she said simply.

"Okay?" Locke's eyes mirrored the conflict raging within him. Ashlee watched him and said nothing. Finally a slight smile tilted the corners of his mouth. "Okay," he murmured. His hand began to move up and down her arm in a rhythmic caress. "Ashlee, I'd like to show you my lab . . . if you still want to see it?"

Ashlee smiled and nodded, feeling almost giddy with relief. Despite the turbulent past hour, Locke still wanted to be with her. And then she remembered his promise to Amber and doubt flickered in her eyes. Was he swallowing his true feelings and sticking with her simply to honor his promise to keep her out of the way?

Locke gazed into her eyes and misinterpreted what he saw there. "Ashlee, I don't blame you for being angry with me. However it happened to occur, you were right, there really were two boys trapped in an elevator and you cared enough to find them. I shouldn't have taunted you, mocked you the way I did. Whatever my feelings, I should have kept my mouth shut."

"I don't want you to feel that you can't speak your mind around me, Locke." Ashlee's heart seemed to have sprouted wings and was soaring with elation. Locke didn't have to apologize to her; *that* wasn't included in his promise to Amber. He didn't have to do it, but he had, of his own volition. Feeling ridiculously happy, she threw him a playful grin. "But you did sound suspiciously like your brother Bryce at one point," she teased him. "And your little crack about the fairies was a rather cheap shot. Imaginative, but cheap."

"I really am sorry, Ashlee," Locke replied somberly. "I—don't want to hurt you."

"I was only teasing you, Locke," Ashlee hastened to explain. She threw up her hands in a display of mock exaggeration and laughed. "We certainly are careful with each other, aren't we? Explaining every remark—"

"Maybe we have to be for a while, Ashlee," Locke interrupted. "Until we know each other better." He smiled down at her and the warmth flowed between them like a tangible force. "But if we're talking cheap shots, comparing me to my brother Bryce is even cheaper than my nasty little fairy story." His eyes gleamed with humor.

"Uh-oh, now it's my turn to apologize!" Ashlee giggled.

Locke swung an arm around her waist and hugged her to his side. "Are we going to stand here trading apologies all afternoon or are you going to have your very first tour of a physics lab?"

Eight

Locke was clearly in his element in the complicated world of thermodynamic physics. He showed Ashlee innumerable charts and graphs, computers and programs and printouts, while he talked on at length about constants and conversion factors and units of electromotive force. His eyes fairly glowed with enthusiasm. Ashlee enjoyed listening to him, although her comprehension of the subject was so vague that she knew she had a long way to go before she even reached the stage of knowing what half of the words he was using meant.

But she liked the alert intelligence that shone in Locke's eyes as he discussed his work, and she could relate to his boundless enthusiasm for his topic. It was important for people to have work that they loved, be it physics or dollmaking. She could identify with and appreciate his absorbing interest in his field. She felt the same sense of excitement and satisfaction when she created a new doll model that Locke was displaying over his homogeneous systems and the isothermal diminution of free energy principle. She watched and listened, her eyes warm with affection as his words swirled over her head.

Locke looked up from a table of graphs and caught her gaze. He drew a breath suddenly and stopped in mid-sentence. "I've been rattling on for the past twenty-five minutes," he said, not seeming able to take his gaze from her face. "You must be thoroughly bored."

Ashlee's smile deepened. "Do I look bored?"

"No." Locke shook his head. "No, you don't." In one swift, sudden movement he lifted her off her feet and set her on one of the long, high tables. He insinuated himself between her knees, his hands resting lightly on her waist "Can I test you on the material that's just been covered, Miss Martin?"

Ashlee gazed into his vivid eyes. "You can test me on anything you want to, Dr. Aames," she whispered, stroking the side of his neck with her fingertips. She ran her fingers through his springy, thick hair, inhaling the masculine scent that was all his own, an intriguing combination of soap and skin and aftershave.

"Oh, Ashlee," Locke said huskily. "Give me your mouth, sweetheart. I want it. I need it."

Ashlee's eyelids closed at the touch of his mouth and she was catapulted into a whirl of dark velvet sensation. Locke's lips moved tantalizingly over hers, and she felt the tip of his tongue seeking entrance to her inner softness. Her lips parted and his tongue penetrated her mouth, seeking and probing. Her tongue rubbed seductively against his, encouraging, challenging it to an erotic little duel. He accepted the challenge with a muffled groan.

Their coats had been discarded on another table shortly after entering the lab, so when Ashlee instinctively pressed closer to Locke, there was no down-filled barrier between them. However, the sparks of static electricity generated by the touching of their sweaters caused them to spring apart in surprise.

"Flying sparks," Ashlee murmured, tracing the line of his jaw with her thumb. "Is there an equation to explain it, Dr. Aames?"

"I'm still investigating the phenomenon," Locke said, breathing a little heavily. "It happens every time I take you in my arms." He brushed his lips lightly over the top of her head. "In the next stages I expect to hear bells ringing and to feel the earth move."

"That's romantic, Locke." She kissed his chin, his forehead, and the tip of his nose.

"You sound surprised." Locke's teeth nipped gently at the soft flesh of her earlobe. "Did you think we physicists were totally lacking the molecules necessary for romance?" His soft laughter seemed to heighten the intimacy between them. He pressed her closer to his lean body.

"Romance molecules, hmm? Discovered in this very physics lab, no doubt?"

"Absolutely."

"Well, I admit that I've always thought physics and romance were poles apart," Ashlee teased lovingly. "And the notion of a romantic physicist seemed as unlikely as a snowstorm in August. But you've proved me wrong, Locke."

Locke pulled her blouse from the waistband of her slacks and slipped his hands beneath her sweater and blouse to touch her skin. "No, you were the one to prove me wrong, my darling Ashlee," he whispered as his lips skimmed over hers. "Until I met you I never connected my biological urges with thoughts and emotions. But with you"—his hand stroked her bare back and her skin felt as if it were aflame—"it's all come together for me, Ashlee. You bring out feelings in me that I never dreamed of experiencing, something that I never believed could exist in me."

"Oh, Locke." Ashlee sighed deeply. She wrapped

herself around Locke and moved sinuously against his body. His hands moved upward to cup the rounded fullness of her breasts, and she gave a small moan of pleasure.

He pulled gently on her nipples, running his fingers up and down over them, and they tightened, almost painfully hard. "You want me," Locke murmured with husky delight, "as much as I want you. Say it, sweetheart. I want to hear you say the words."

"I want you, Locke," Ashlee admitted, reeling in the erotic dream he was creating. The voluptuous emotions surging through her went far beyond mere sexual excitement. There was something primitive and elemental in her overwhelming response to Locke Aames. He was the only man to have ever evoked such a shattering effect upon all of her senses.

"And I want you, Ashlee. I need you so much." Locke withdrew his hands from her breasts, and his arms encircled her possessively. Ashlee thrust against him, wanting him to touch her, aching for it. He held her tightly, but he didn't touch her where she wanted to be touched and he didn't kiss her. Ashlee wriggled and writhed, but he kept control of her, holding her and whispering softly to her.

Eventually Ashlee felt the taut sexual tension begin to drain from their bodies, and she was grateful for Locke's restraint. Had he not stopped, she would have willingly allowed him to make love to her right there in the physics lab. Her cheeks flamed at the thought. "I—I don't know what to say," she confessed. "You must think that I—"

"I think you are the most exciting, passionate, and desirable woman I've ever met," Locke interrupted swiftly. "And I want our first time together to be perfect, Ashlee, not in the sterile, scientific atmosphere of a laboratory."

Ashlee relaxed in his arms, her eyes closed, feeling incredibly close to him. "You are a romantic, Locke," she whispered, and clung closer.

When they finally and reluctantly drew apart, they gazed into each other's eyes, freely revealing the intensity of their emotions. Impulsively Ashlee gave Locke a quick hug and jumped down from the table. "We'd better get out of here, professor, before we're caught by one of your colleagues, or worse, your dreaded undergraduates."

"Ashlee, I . . ." Locke paused, his eyes never leaving her. "I'd be proud to introduce you to any one of them."

Her heart quickened. "Thank you, Locke."

They walked back to the car hand in hand. The wind had died down and though the sky was gray and threatening and the temperature hadn't risen a single degree, Ashlee didn't feel the chill. She was warmed by the heat of her body's inner glow.

"Shall we drive into Boston?" Locke asked as they climbed into the car. "We can decide where we're going to have dinner and—oh, hell!" He cursed the silence that followed the turn of the key in the ignition. "A dead battery!" He pumped the gas pedal and turned the key again. Again, nothing. "I can't believe it, this battery is only a year old. I'm sorry about this, honey. I'll call the automobile club to come out and jump-start the car."

"Why don't we take a look under the hood first?" Ashlee suggested.

"Why bother? A dead battery looks the same as a live one. Do you want to wait here in the car or come back to my office with me while I call triple A?"

"It might not be the battery, though. Unlock your hood and I'll have a look."

"Oh, come on, Ashlee, you don't—"

She leaned over and pulled the small handle that released the lock to the car's hood. A moment later Ashlee was surveying the engine. "Hmm." Her gaze swept over the parts and she touched a few of them. Locke hovered behind her, watching. Her fingers closed around a cap and she quickly tightened it. "The alternator cap was loose. Try to start it now."

Locke's jaw dropped. He remained standing beside the car, saying nothing.

"Start it up. I'll stand out here and watch." Locke slowly climbed back into the car. Seconds later the engine roared to life. Ashlee closed the hood with a slam and bounded back into the car.

"You fixed it," Locke said, thunderstruck. "How did you know what to do?"

"My uncles and some of my cousins are the real whiz mechanics," Ashlee confided modestly. "I only know how to fix simple, obvious problems. My cousin Otis is only twenty-one and he can fix any car, foreign or domestic. He's thinking of opening his own garage in Durham or Chapel Hill in a few years."

"I see. Can you change a tire too?"

"Of course. My Uncle Billy wouldn't let any of us get our driver's license until we knew how to change a tire and do minor repairs." She couldn't quite interpret Locke's expression. "Does it bother you, Locke? Do you mind?" she asked softly.

"Why should I mind? I think it's fantastic. We didn't have to call the automobile club and wait around for them to arrive. And I firmly believe that every woman who drives a car should know how to change a flat tire. Mother and Amber were once stranded with a flat for four and a half hours on the Connecticut Turnpike. They could do nothing but sit and wait for a patrol car to come to their assistance. But I wouldn't have to worry about you on the road," he added thoughtfully, looking pleased. "And if I were ever incapacitated and we had a flat, you could change it and we would be on our way."

"That's a level-headed and liberal viewpoint," Ashlee said, happily surprised. "Some men have the most peculiar hang-ups about women and cars. Steve Walton, for instance. He had a conniption fit when I changed a flat tire on his car because he—uh—didn't know how to work the jack. He resented the fact that I did."

"What a boob! And you actually entertained the idea of marrying such a chauvinistic idiot?"

Ashlee grinned. "Someday he'll be a well-to-do radiologist. My friend Sandy thinks he'll be a terrific husband."

"Then Sandy can marry him. You certainly aren't, Ashlee."

"No." She stared at Locke, her brown eyes luminous. "I'm not."

"Well, I'm glad that's settled." Locke backed the Olds out of the parking space. "And I don't care to hear any more anecdotes about the would-be radiologist either."

"Yes, sir!" Ashlee gave him a mock salute. "Any other orders, sir?"

"Just one. Come and sit closer to me."

They spent an idyllic evening together. Dinner was at The Romagnolis' Table in Boston's Faneuil Hall Marketplace. They were delighted to learn that, however far apart most of their food preferences might be, they both loved lasagna. They lingered over dessert—rum cake and spumoni for Ashlee, Italian ice for Locke—for a long time, holding hands across the table, gazing into each other's eyes, and talking about everything and nothing at all. Ashlee paid the check without further demur from Locke. He inspected her credit card and teased her about putting his meal on her expense account. She assured him that she didn't have one. "I had to make four or five dolls to cover the cost of your dinner," she retorted. "That's why I made you clean your plate."

It was nearly ten-thirty when they returned to the Aames house, and they'd just stepped inside the door when Sharon, wearing pajamas, robe, and slippers, raced down the stairs. "Hi, Ashlee! Hi, Uncle Locke!"

Locke groaned and looked at his watch. "Aren't you supposed to be in bed?"

Sharon ignored him. "The phone's been ringing off the wall tonight, Ashlee. You get as many phone calls as I do," she added in an admiring tone.

Ashlee tensed and felt Locke stiffen beside her.

"I wrote them all down." Sharon fished in the pocket of her robe and pulled out a piece of crumpled note paper. "Here's the list, and everyone wants you to call them back. Your grandmother, Sandy Marshall, Steve Walton, Lori Charleston, and Garrison Kramer." She handed Ashlee the paper. "You can use the phone in my room if you want, Ashlee."

"There's no need for that." Locke plucked the list from Ashlee's fingers and read it, frowning. "She'll use the telephone in the den. And it's time you were in bed, Sharon."

"Trying to get rid of me, huh?" Sharon grinned cheekily.

"Not at all," Ashlee said, smiling. "Thanks for your offer, Sharon, but I will use the phone in the den. And thank you for being my answering service tonight."

"Garrison Kramer called twice," Sharon said, "but I only marked him down once on the list. He said he'd tried to reach you three other times during the day." Her eyes grew round. "Hey, isn't he the guy who Aunt Amber went out with?"

"Good night, Sharon," Locke said firmly.

"He is!" exclaimed Sharon. "Uh-oh!"

"Up!" Locke pointed to the staircase. "Immediately!"

"Now I know why you want Ashlee to use the phone in the den—so you can listen in." Sharon sauntered toward the stairs. "Well, my offer still stands, Ashlee. 'Night."

Ashlee wished she could think of a reason to prolong the girl's stay, but none came to mind. "Good night, Sharon."

"Good riddance," Locke muttered under his breath. "She used to be such a charming child."

"She still is." Ashlee cast him a covert glance. He was staring at the list, his expression grim. The aura of warmth and companionship that had enveloped them throughout the evening had evaporated. She made a stab at regaining it. "I'll have to call Gran first. She's probably bursting to know all about Amber. And Sandy will be too. But I can't imagine why Lori called me." Although she carefully avoided mentioning Steve and Garrison Kramer, their unspoken names hung between them.

Locke handed her the piece of paper, which he had wadded into a ball. "Maybe Lori is searching for buried treasure and wants you to pinpoint the exact location on a map," he suggested sarcastically, and Ashlee suppressed a sigh. So they were back to square one.

"Locke, I didn't ask Steve Walton or Garrison Kramer to call me."

"Did I say that you did?"

"No, but you're angry and I assume that's why."

"Did I say I was angry?"

Ashlee heaved an exasperated groan. "Locke, your style of arguing leaves a lot to be desired. If you're mad because they called me, then tell me so. Say, 'Dammit, Ashlee, I don't like other men calling you and please don't return their calls.' "

Locke carefully arranged his coat on a hanger and hung it in the hall closet. "Is that what you want me to say, Ashlee?"

Ashlee clenched her fists. "One more of your parroty questions, Locke Aames, and I'll—"

"And you'll what?"

"That's it!" Ashlee stormed. Impossible man! Did he think she would stand there and let him bait her all night? "If you'll excuse me, I'll make these calls." She headed for the den, fuming. What nerve! She'd bent over backward to appease his overly sensitive male ego and he'd thrown her words back in her face. Her anger doubled with righteous indignation, and she paused to call over her shoulder, "And don't worry that I'll run up your telephone bill with long distance calls. I intend to call collect."

"That's good to know." He wouldn't even let her have the last parting shot. "I was really worried about that, Ashlee. Yes, make sure you make your long distance calls collect."

Tossed back at her, her little jibe sounded as ineffectual as Locke's juvenile questions. Ashlee glowered at him. "Do you always have to have the last word?"

"Do you?"

"Yes!" She lifted her chin haughtily and marched into the den.

To Sandy and Steve, Ashlee painted a glowing picture of Amber's reception and their warm sisterly togetherness. She told them how much she loved Aames, Massachusetts, and no, it wasn't all *that* cold here. When Steve asked when she was coming back, she gave no definite departure date. Ashlee could practically hear him sulking across the miles and her own mood did not improve. When Steve reminded her that the chief of radiology was throwing his annual January dinner dance the next Saturday and that he planned to attend with a date, whether she had returned to Chapel Hill or not, Ashlee told him to have a good time. Steve began to mutter the name of Janice Dixon, the pretty assistant head nurse in the cardiac care unit. Ashlee flippantly wished him good luck with her. By the time the call ended, they weren't on the best of terms.

Ashlee was a bit more candid with her grandmother. "Amber and I are very, very different, Gran," she said slowly. Sudden tears filled her eyes and she blinked them away. She was well aware that she wanted to cry over Amber *and* Locke Aames. "I—I think it's going to take time for her to . . . accept me."

"Then give her that time, Ashlee. Once she gets to know you, she'll love you," Gran said warmly. "Everybody loves my little girl."

It was exactly what she'd expected Gran to say, but Ashlee had her doubts. A doting grandmother wasn't exactly an impartial observer.

She called Lori Charleston next. Apparently Lori had been so excited to meet a bona fide clairvoyant with lab test credentials that she'd telephoned her parapsychology instructor that morning. He wanted Lori to extend an invitation to Ashlee to visit the class one day that week; the instructor intended to call himself tomorrow. The Aameses were going to love that, Ashlee thought, grimacing. Herself as Exhibit A in a junior college parapsychology class. She told Lori that she'd have to give the matter some thought.

She had put off calling Garrison Kramer till last. Staring at his number on Sharon's list, Ashlee arrived at a decision. She would *not* return his call. Surely he would take a hint from such an obvious, direct snub.

The phone began to ring as she climbed the stairs to her bedroom. "Ashlee," Locke called from the kitchen. His tone was as frozen as the spumoni she'd had for dessert. "Telephone for you." He handed her the receiver as she entered the kitchen. "Sharon might enjoy playing answering service, but I don't." He stalked out of the kitchen, leaving behind a half full glass of ice water.

Ashlee knew who was on the line before she ever heard Garrison Kramer's voice. Locke's thunderous expression had been a dead giveaway. She stuck her tongue out at the telephone receiver and wished Garrison Kramer could see her reaction to his call.

"You're a very difficult lady to reach," came Kramer's admiring voice when she said hello.

"There is a reason for that," Ashlee replied frostily. What kind of a man was this? He had been dating her sister, her twin sister! Did he actually expect her to blithely sanction his defection from Amber to her?

It seemed that he did. He wanted to take her to dinner the next evening. And he had tickets to a play the night after that. Ashlee's temper ignited and blazed. Not only had this man hurt Amber and jeopardized a chance for friendship between her and her twin, he had also caused a rift between her and Locke. The more Ashlee thought about it, the angrier she grew. If they'd been in Shade Gap, she would have set the dogs on Garrison Kramer. Instead, she had to settle for words to convey her wrath.

"I'm going to tell you this only once, Mr. Kramer, so listen carefully. I don't want you calling me again. I have no intention of seeing you or dating you or even talking to you, ever again. Any man who tries to come between sisters holds as much appeal as—as hog slop!" She heard him spluttering on the other end of the line and proceeded to drive her point home. "I don't like you and I never will. Your treatment of my sister makes me your permanent enemy. I can't stand the thought of you, Garrison Kramer. Have I made myself clear?" She banged the receiver back into its cradle, well aware that the hapless Kramer had taken the brunt of the day's frustration. Well, too bad! He'd had it coming, trying to switch twins.

Having expended her anger, Ashlee felt calmer, and her thoughts focused quite naturally on Locke and their spat. Locke had been jealous and she hadn't helped matters by taking the heat herself.

She could have reassured him, made a joke of Steve's and Kramer's calls. Locke had confessed that he was a stranger to the strong emotions she roused in him; Ashlee was willing to bet that experiencing jealousy over a woman was totally new to him. New and unpleasant. No wonder he had lashed out at her, pretending to shrug her off without a care. It was far easier to retreat behind a façade of indifference than to confront such powerful foreign feelings. Her gaze came to rest upon the glass of ice water Locke had left behind. A man shouldn't have to go to bed thirsty. She would take the glass of water to his room and . . .

Ashlee stood at the top of the stairs and gazed down the darkened hallway, trying to remember which room was Locke's. The third or the fourth door on the right? All she needed was to surprise Alec in his bedroom by mistake.

"Ashlee?"

Amber's sudden appearance startled Ashlee so much that she jumped, sloshing water over her hand and onto the carpet. "Amber!"

Amber's face was grim. "I'd—I'd like to talk to you, if I may."

"Of course, Amber."

"Come into my room." Amber walked ahead and Ashlee followed her into her bedroom. Amber closed the door behind them. "Ashlee, this isn't easy for me to say," she began, and swallowed hard.

Why, she was nervous, Ashlee noted with surprise. Cool, self-possessed Amber . . . nervous because of her? Ashlee tried to give her sister her most encouraging, supportive smile. "Please don't be afraid to tell me anything, Amber."

"I overheard your telephone conversation with Garrison Kramer," Amber blurted out. "When the phone rang I picked it up at the same time Locke did. When I heard Garry's voice asking for you I—I stayed on the line. I know it was reprehensible of me, but I couldn't seem to bring myself to hang up."

·"Then you heard what I told him," Ashlee said calmly.

Amber nodded and suddenly, unexpectedly, began to laugh. "Oh, Ashlee, hog slop! I nearly died!" With that, the ice was well and truly broken, the lines of communication open at last.

"I meant every word I said to him, Amber. I hate the way he's treated you. Anyone who hurts my sister can never be a friend of mine."

Amber sank down onto one of the twin beds. "I was so sure you would go out with him and—and fall in love with him. I could see how much he admired you."

"Fall in love with that jerk? Come on, Amber! The man is as desirable as tooth decay."

"Ashlee, no," Amber protested somewhere between laughter and tears. "Garry is handsome and well-dressed. He's the most popular man at the branch bank in Cambridge."

"And that's why you like him? This sounds like a replay of my crush on the captain of the junior high school basketball team."

"Oh, I know! I have absolutely nothing in common with him other than the fact that he works for the bank. I don't know what's come over me in the past few months, Ashlee. My sudden interest in Garrison Kramer was so untypical of me. I've never been all that interested in"—Amber blushed and looked at the floor—"in the opposite sex. I've always been too busy with my studies, too sensible for that sort of thing. Ashlee, I never had crushes when I was a teenager. Imagine my horror in finding myself mooning over Garrison Kramer like some love-struck adolescent! I—I reminded myself of Sharon!"

Ashlee sat beside her on the bed. "Gran says that nobody skips a stage of development. It sounds like you're now going through what you managed to skip as a teenager."

"I wasn't a typical teenager, nothing at all like Sharon with her music and her gang of friends and her crushes every other week," Amber conceded with a sad smile. "I worried incessantly about my grades. My brothers were brilliant students—Locke was exceptionally gifted—and I wanted so much to measure up to them. I had no time for silly adolescent pastimes . . . and I had no friends either. I still don't, Ashlee."

"Oh, Amber," Ashlee said softly, putting her arms around her sister.

Amber began to cry. "I've been unhappy for such a long time, Ashlee. I've never felt that I really belonged anywhere. I wasn't really an Aames, though I tried hard to be. But every time I looked at the pictures of the baby girl who died, the *real* Aames daughter, I . . ." Her voice trailed off.

"What pictures?" prompted Ashlee.

"When I was about six I found a packet of color snapshots in my mother's drawer. Oh, I know I shouldn't have been going through her bureau, but I was looking for pennies and I came across those pictures. I've never told anyone about them. In one of the pictures, the baby, she was named Martha Cordelia after both grandmothers, was dressed in a long christening gown and bonnet and was lying in a little white coffin. I later learned that it was the christening dress that had been used by generations of Aames babies, including my brothers. They buried little Martha Cordelia in it. After I was adopted, the family had a special christening ceremony for me. There are pictures of me in a brand-new dress." Amber shrugged and sniffled. "Well, why not? I wasn't born an Aames, I wasn't a part of the family's traditions. I was new, an alien. Baby Martha was the real Aames daughter with the family christening gown and both grandmothers' names. I got the new, traditionless dress and the meaningless name, made up for me by the woman who gave me away."

"And you've spent your life feeling like an outsider, sort of a substitute for the lost baby," Ashlee said.

"An inadequate substitute," Amber corrected her. "It's insane, isn't it? Feeling jealous of a poor dead infant?"

"I don't think it's insane," Ashlee said soothingly. "But there is something you seem to have forgotten, Amber. The baby might have been given the heirloom dress and the grandmother's names, but you've had the life she didn't. You were given a future, Amber."

For a few minutes the sisters sat in silence as Amber struggled to regain her composure. When she'd wiped away the last of her tears she took Ashlee's hand. "Ashlee, I want you to understand that none of this is my parents' fault. They've been wonderful to me, honestly. They never insisted on the high grades; I was the one who set impossibly high standards for myself. I was the one who practiced for hours on the flute so I could be as good as the rest of the family. They just wanted me to play it for pleasure," she added quietly.

"Locke mentioned the Aames family band."

"The Aameses all have natural musical ability." Amber sighed. "But I don't have one iota. I have to practice five times as hard and I still lack their fluency and flair. They all have wonderful singing voices too. I can barely carry a tune. Can you, Ashlee?"

"Not at all," confessed Ashlee. "I love to sing, but I'm horrendously off-key. The children's choir director in Shade Gap used to bribe me not to sing with the other kids on Sundays. She'd give me gum and candy if I just mouthed the words to the hymns."

"Poor Ashlee! Weren't you crushed?"

"Oh, no. I felt lucky because I was the only kid in

the choir to get a bag of treats every week. I looked forward to it."

"That's the difference between you and me, Ashlee. I would have been devastated. I've always felt lacking in every way."

"And now you're working in the Aames bank like Bryce and Alec to please your father," Ashlee said. "And you're working on your MBA at Harvard, their alma mater. Are you happy with your work, or is it just more in the way of compensation for not being Martha Cordelia?"

Two pairs of identical brown eyes met and held. "Ashlee, I—I can trust you, can't I?" Amber took a deep breath, considering her own question. "You came all this way to find me and you refused to go out with Garrison Kramer."

Ashlee squeezed her twin's hand. "You can trust me, Amber."

"I've never told this to another living soul." Amber was trembling with the force of her emotions. "Ashlee, I—I—I hate the bank!" Her voice shook. "And I hate the Harvard Business School! And most of all—most of all—I hate my flute."

Ashlee could only guess what an effort it had been for her sister to utter those words. She gave her a firm, compassionate hug. "Amber, have you ever thought of quitting the bank?"

"Oh, no, I couldn't!" Amber gasped, shocked at the suggestion. "It's my career, my future. What would I do with my life?"

"Change it. Come back to North Carolina with me. We could find out who Amber Aames really is, what she likes and doesn't like. There would be no pressure, no expectations. You could live in my apartment with me and we'll go to Shade Gap and visit my family, the Martins. They'll love you, Amber. My grandmother has already told me that she considers my twin sister another granddaughter."

Amber stood up and began to gnaw her thumbnail nervously. Just like me, Ashlee noted, touched by the shared bad habit. "It's a very generous offer, Ashlee, but . . ."

"Amber, I mean it. Every word! Quit business school and the bank. Throw away your stupid flute and come to Chapel Hill with me."

"Throw away my stupid flute?" Amber echoed. Then she giggled. "My stupid flute!" A moment later she was laughing uproariously, her slim shoulders shaking.

Ashlee joined in her laughter, joy singing through her. This was the way she had always dreamed it would be. She and her twin sister together, sharing confidences and laughter and tears. "Oh, Amber, I wish I'd found you years ago!"

"I do too, Ashlee." Amber was suddenly serious. "Ever since I was a child I've felt—I've known—that something was missing from my life. Maybe it was you, Ashlee. My twin sister."

The twins embraced. It was one of the most beautiful moments of her life, Ashlee thought, tears of happiness in her eyes. Her long search had finally ended.

Nine

"Ashlee, there's something else that I have to tell you," Amber said as she and Ashlee sat at the kitchen table drinking cocoa. Ashlee had made it from scratch, refusing even to try the sugar-free hot water mix. The twins had decided that sleep was impossible; both were eager to begin the important task of learning all about each other.

"What is it, Amber?"

"I've done something very unfair, something that I'm terribly ashamed of. . . ." Amber played with the handle of her cup. "Ashlee, this morning when Garry called you, I felt so jealous and so spiteful that I—I asked Locke to keep you away from the house so that Garry couldn't reach you. And—oh, Ashlee, this sounds awful and I hope you'll be able to forgive me—but I asked Locke to feign an interest in you in hopes of diverting your attention from Garrison Kramer."

"I know," Ashlee said calmly. "We seem to share a common interest in eavesdropping, Amber."

Amber gulped. "You heard?"

"I was outside the kitchen door. I wanted to tell

you that you had nothing to fear from me, but I thought you wouldn't believe me."

"I probably wouldn't have. Ashlee, I'm sorry for not trusting you and I'm sorry I took advantage of Locke's loyalty in that way. It was wrong, I know."

"I had a wonderful time today, Amber, and I wasn't under any illusions as to why Locke invited me," Ashlee assured Amber, but her heart was sinking fast. Sometime between their lovemaking in the physics lab and dinner in Boston she'd managed to forget Locke's promise to Amber. Amber's halting confession painfully refreshed her memory.

"I wasn't thinking straight when I asked Locke to do it," Amber said, sinking back into her chair. "I was so upset that Garrison had actually called you. You see, I was the one to ask him out on all three of our dates." Her face flushed scarlet. "He never reciprocated."

"We're just going to forget the whole thing, Amber," Ashlee said, forcing her brightest smile. It was difficult to swallow around the lump that was forming in her throat. "Particularly that insignificant speck, Garrison Kramer. No harm has been done, after all."

Except that she'd fallen wildly in love with Locke Aames, Ashlee amended silently. But that wasn't Amber's fault. She'd been halfway there on her own since the first time he'd kissed her.

"Thank you for being so understanding, Ashlee," Amber murmured. In another moment they'd both be crying again, Ashlee realized, seeing the tears in Amber's eyes and feeling them in her own. It was time to inject a little levity into the conversation. "And you don't have to worry that I'm going to try to con you out of your fortune either. I'm fresh out of extortion plots this month," she teased.

"You heard *that* too?" Amber wailed. "Oh, Ashlee, I never thought any such thing. Sometimes Bryce can be so pigheaded and paranoid. I'm embarrassed beyond words."

"Don't be. I had no business spying, anyway."

"What's going on in here?" Alec Aames bounded into the kitchen, vitally attractive in a three-piece gray suit. "Is this a private party or can I come too?"

"You're home early, Alec," Amber said, glancing at the wall clock. "You haven't come in at midnight since you were in the ninth grade."

"It was an extremely dull party." Alec dipped a spoon into the pan of hot chocolate and tasted it. "And I'm only temporarily in. Cynthia invited me over to her place for—uh—dessert. She had another date to get rid of too."

Amber rolled her eyes. "Isn't it tiring, Alec? Being a lady-killer?"

"Never." Alec flashed his incredibly white teeth. "Don't hold breakfast for me, sweetie. Good night, twins." He gave each a brotherly pat on the head and departed.

"Two dates in one night," Amber said, shaking her head. "His social life has never ceased to amaze me."

"Locke and Bryce aren't as social?" Ashlee asked, her voice carefully casual.

"Bryce has had a date almost every weekend since his divorce, but I don't think he really enjoys himself. He sees it as a kind of revenge against Nancy, who couldn't care less." Amber smiled wryly. "And Locke doesn't go out all that much. He's had relationships, of course, but strictly on his own terms and at his convenience. I think he's too cerebral and too logical to become passionately involved with anyone."

Ashlee took a long swallow of her hot chocolate. Until tonight her goal in life had been to find her twin and establish the relationship denied them by their separate adoptions. Having achieved that, she realized a new, even more powerful ambition simmering within her and fueled by Amber's words. She wanted the too cerebral, too logical Locke Aames to be passionately involved with her. Permanently.

"But I don't want you to think that Locke is unfeeling or uncaring," Amber was saying warmly. "He's always been my favorite brother. Locke was the one who always made time for me. He taught me to ride a two-wheeler when I was six and how to drive at sixteen. I want the two of you to be really good friends."

"So do I, Amber. So do I." Really good friends and much, much more, Ashlee added silently.

A loud, off-key version of an old Cole Porter standard brought the conversation to an abrupt stop. The voice rose an octave and launched into an appalling refrain. The twins looked at each other and burst into laughter. "Who is that?" Ashlee asked. "At last I've found someone who sings worse than I do."

"Mrs. Bates. Sounds like she's back from her lost weekend." Amber chuckled. "She's been the cook for the family for the past twenty-seven years. Unfortunately she's been drunk for the past ten of them."

"Does she cook as badly as she sings? No wonder you Aameses have such weird tastes in food."

"Mother and Dad don't have the heart to fire her. She has no family and nowhere else to go. She has a small room and bath down the back hall from the kitchen." Amber shook her head, her eyes brimming with laughter. "My parents did make her stop smoking her horrible little cigars though. The kitchen used to reek of them."

"She smokes cigars?" Ashlee whooped. "Sounds like a Yankee Mammy Yokum!" The two sisters dissolved into laughter.

It wasn't until much later that Ashlee and Amber

said their final good nights and headed to their respective bedrooms. They had been talking non-stop about their childhoods and their adoptive families and their present-day lives. Ashlee entered her darkened bedroom and groped her way to the chair by the radiator, where she'd purposefully draped her nightgown. It would be warm from the radiator heat and, after the previous night in this icy chamber, Ashlee knew she needed all the warmth she could muster.

She quickly stripped off all her clothes, letting them fall into a small pile at her feet. She was reaching for the heated nightgown when a light was switched on, bathing the room in a dim glow. Ashlee uttered a breathless little shriek. Locke was in the bed, under the covers, his hand on the switch of the bedside lamp. His dark hair was tousled and he looked as if he'd just awakened from sleep.

For a few stunned seconds the two of them stared at each other, motionless. Then Ashlee snatched her nightgown and held it in front of her. "W-what are you doing here?" she managed to choke.

"No, don't cover yourself," Locke said hoarsely, throwing back the covers and walking over to her. He wore only white cotton briefs. "You have a beautiful body, Ashlee." He tugged at the nightgown, which she was holding like a shield. "I want to see you, sweetheart. All of you. Please . . . please, love."

His sensual plea melted all resistance within her. Ashlee's eyes held his as she released her grip on the nightgown. Locke took it from her and tossed it back onto the chair. "You are beautiful, Ashlee," he said, gazing at her raptly. "I knew you would be."

His urgency was affecting her like a potent drug, making her senses swim. Ashlee reached out to touch the soft hair that covered his chest. "You're beautiful too, Locke," she breathed. Locke lifted her hand to his lips and pressed his mouth against her palm. "I knew you would say that." He chuckled huskily. "You're always telling me how handsome and sexy I am. You make me feel like it's really true. When I'm with you I feel like the most desirable man in the world."

"You are," Ashlee whispered.

"Only with you, love. And only for you." The hot flames in his eyes were melting her, and her body throbbed in response. It seemed the most natural thing in the world for Ashlee to move into his arms.

"I've been waiting here for you." He blazed a trail of hungry kisses along the curve of her neck. "I want to tell you something, Ashlee." He cupped the swollen softness of her full breasts. The nipples were already pointed and hard. When he flicked his thumb over one, a great shudder of desire tore through her.

"What do you want to tell me, Locke?" Ashlee heard herself ask in a ragged, faraway voice.

"Just this. Dammit, Ashlee, I don't like other men calling you and I hate it even more when you return their calls." His hand slid possessively over the smooth curve of her belly and her stomach contracted at his touch. "I was so damn jealous of those two men that I lashed out at you," he murmured ruefully. "It's all so new to me, Ashlee, the jealousy, the possessiveness." His lips moved slowly, sensuously, from her neck to her breast. "And the passion . . ."

His voice trailed off as his tongue found her nipple. He traced concentric circles around it until it stood out, far and hard. A hungry little moan escaped from deep in her throat. "I want to make love to you, Ashlee. I need you so badly." Locke's hand slid lower to the downy softness at the apex of her thighs.

Liquid fire churned through her veins, and the tension in the pit of her abdomen was an exquisite ache. She could feel the hardness of his masculinity against her and knew the strength and power of his arousal. Her heart blazed with the desire to give and give to him. There was something incredibly enticing in the urgency of his need for her. Ashlee felt the heady combination of tenderness and feminine power as she clung to him. He needed her, wanted her so desperately. And she was so in love with him. Why even try to resist what they both wanted, what they both needed? Why not succumb to the unique passion that was theirs alone?

"Oh, yes, Locke," she whispered, and Locke lifted her into his arms. Ashlee pressed her face into the curve of his shoulder, her pulse pounding at a frantic pace. He carried her to the bed and laid her down on it. Dreamily she watched him peel off his briefs and come to her, and she welcomed him with open arms. It felt so very right to give herself to the man she loved. Locke's hands swept over the soft curves of her body, and a hot flood of anticipation flowed through her.

"You're mine, Ashlee," Locke said hoarsely, his eyes intense as they gazed into hers. His long fingers brushed the sensitive, intimate warmth of her and Ashlee drew a deep breath. "And tonight I'm going to show you how completely you belong to me."

Ashlee was trembling uncontrollably as his fingers teased, reaching close to her throbbing core, tantalizing her with a too brief caress and then drawing away. "Please, Locke." Her voice was as husky as his. Her fingers closed around his wrist and she guided his hand back to her.

"Yes, love," Locke crooned, touching her. "We're going to be so good together."

Ashlee's body was taut with the agony of wanting him, and when Locke's mouth closed over hers with compelling possession, she surrendered completely to the intense loving passion and mutual need. Both were drawn into the mindless, swirling vortex of pleasure and passion that merged them and made them one.

• • •

Ashlee snuggled deeper into Locke's arms, savoring their newfound intimacy in the soothing afterglow of passion. She felt relaxed and content, blissfully happy and deeply in love. I love you, she told Locke over and over again in her mind, wondering if she dared to speak the words aloud. She didn't want him to feel obliged to parrot the phrase back to her or to place any undue pressure on him to return her feelings. He would, in time; Ashlee was ever hopeful of that. For now she was satisfied to hold him, treasuring these special moments alone with him.

"How long were you waiting here for me?" she asked drowsily, luxuriating in his firm, sweeping caresses.

"It felt like forever." He kissed her upturned chin. "I saw Amber meet you at the top of the stairs and watched the two of you go into her room. I came into your room a few minutes later. I really did intend to talk to you, Ashlee." He flashed a sudden grin. "I hadn't planned to surprise you in bed à la Red Riding Hood and the wolf. I sat in the chair, fully dressed, for over an hour. When you still hadn't come . . ."

"You decided to lay down for a bit."

"And I was uncomfortable lying in bed with my clothes on."

"And the rest is history." Ashlee paused to kiss him lingeringly. "I'm glad you were here, Locke."

"Oh, honey, so am I." His arms tightened possessively and they kissed again. "Ashlee?" Locke rolled her on top of him and anchored her there with his hands. "You spent a long time with Amber tonight. Have you reached some sort of understanding?"

Ashlee nodded happily. She had her twin sister and Locke. Never had her life seemed more perfect.

"I think Amber and I are going to be close friends as well as sisters, Locke."

"I'm glad, honey." He smiled. "Now it's time for me to put out the light so we can get some sleep, lover." He flicked off the lamp on the bedside table.

"Locke, do you think it's . . . wise to stay here with me all night? Your family might . . ."

"I'm not sneaking out of your bedroom like some cat burglar!" Locke said indignantly, and Ashlee laughed at his obvious outrage. He silenced her with a long, passionate kiss. "I can't leave you, Ashlee. I want you to sleep in my arms. I want to hold you the whole night through."

Ashlee acquiesced with a contented little sigh. "There's just one thing, Locke . . ."

"Honey, forget about my family, they—"

"No, it has nothing to do with your family. I'd like to put on my nightgown. Warm as you are, I still need flannel to survive your frigid Yankee temperatures."

"Frigid?" Locke said. "It's invigorating."

"To polar bears, maybe." She grinned impishly. "Locke, would you mind getting out of bed to fetch my nightgown? You can enjoy the invigorating chill to the fullest."

Locke complied with a good-natured grumble. "The things a man does for his woman! You'll probably have me trooping to the kitchen at three A.M. for strawberries and pickles when you're pregnant."

Ashlee's heart seemed to stop, then start again at an awesome speed. She pictured herself married to Locke, carrying their child. A warm flush spread over her whole body as she contemplated the evocative scene. "Marshmallows and pickles," she corrected him, keeping her tone light. It would suffice if Locke were merely bantering with her. But if he cared to carry the discussion into the serious realm . . . "Much to my heartbreak, I can't eat strawberries." She watched him pick up the nightgown and bring it to her. "They make me break out in hives."

"No kidding? Strawberries have the same effect on Amber." He held the nightgown while Ashlee wriggled into it. He seemed perfectly content to let the subject of her hypothetical pregnancy drop. Instead, she found herself being regaled with various Aames family members' allergies and aversions. She finally forced a wide yawn. "Oh, I'm so sleepy," she said apologetically, a trifle ashamed at the lie. Had Locke chosen to pursue the topic of their future together, she could have willingly talked the night away. But who wanted to hear about Grandfather Aames's allergy to clams at three o'clock in the morning?

"Of course you are, love," Locke said with such concern that Ashlee felt doubly guilty. "I'll stop talking and let you go to sleep."

"Don't I get a good-night kiss?" Ashlee didn't wait for an answer. She gave him a slow, sweet kiss, pouring all her love and yearning into intense physical expression.

Locke's response was fierce and immediate. "Oh, Ashlee." He moved on top of her. "Do you know what you're doing to me?"

Ashlee felt a tremor pass through his body. She nipped erotically at his shoulder, her fingers digging into the hard muscles of his back. "Locke, I'm not sleepy anymore." She teased him with the slow, sensual rhythm of her hips. Seconds later her nightgown hit the floor. Ashlee felt the heavy strength of him filling her and called his name in an ecstatic little cry.

"You're driving me wild, Ashlee." Locke groaned as he felt her body tighten with a special sensuous tension. "So soft and small, so full of fire and warmth." He surged against her, his breathing ragged. "Let go and come to me, darling. You belong to me in every way."

Ashlee gave herself up to the exhilarating forces

that swept her from wild, uninhibited abandon to rapturous ecstasy. When Locke called her name in a hoarse whisper, she knew he had joined her there.

Settled comfortably in each other's arms, Ashlee's nightgown providing a flannel barrier that Locke sleepily teased her about, they said loving good nights. Locke was asleep within a few minutes and Ashlee lay warm and happy, feeling closer to him than she'd ever felt to anyone. Her eyelids fluttered shut and she felt herself begin to drift off to sleep.

When the scene first appeared before her, Ashlee thought she was dreaming. But when she opened her eyes the image remained. She moaned in protest. Not now! Her mind railed against the timing of that inexplicable awareness known as clairvoyance.

But the scene kept recurring with insistent frequency. She saw a small wastebasket lined with a white plastic bag in a small blue and yellow room, a bathroom. Smoke was rising from the wastebasket. Something was smoldering in it. Ashlee bolted up in bed as a tongue of bright orange flame leaped from the wastebasket to ignite the towel hanging on the bar above it. In a kind of fascinated horror she watched the towel catch fire and burn. There were curtains above the towels. In another minute or two they would also be aflame.

Ashlee glanced at Locke sleeping beside her and recalled with a grimace his reaction to the mere mention of her ESP visions. Their lovemaking and its aftermath had been so wonderful, so perfect, she couldn't bear to poison the atmosphere with the dissension her clairvoyance would raise. If she were to wake him now and tell him that she saw a fire in a trash can . . .

Quietly Ashlee slipped from the bed and groped in the dark for her robe and slippers. Locke was sleeping deeply and did not stir. She left the room and hurried down the hall to Amber's room. There was no time to lose.

A light was shining from beneath the crack of Amber's door. Ashlee knocked and whispered her sister's name. Amber, wearing a flannel nightgown identical to Ashlee's, opened the door. "We're wearing the same nightgown," Amber said with amazement.

"Amber, where is Mrs. Bates's room?" Ashlee asked. She knew as she spoke that the fire was there. "Will you take me to it?" she added urgently.

Amber gave her an odd stare.

"Please, Amber, hurry! There's a fire!"

"A fire?" Amber squeaked. "In Mrs. Bates's room?"

"In her bathroom. Hurry!"

The two sisters raced downstairs, Ashlee following Amber through the smoke-filled kitchen and into a tiny blue and yellow bathroom now thick with smoke. The towel was burning and the curtains had caught fire. "Call the fire department," cried Ashlee, "and find Mrs. Bates. I'll turn on the shower and wet some towels and try to put out the fire."

"Ashlee, be careful!" Amber squeezed her hand.

After summoning the fire department and leading a groggy Mrs. Bates into the front hall, Amber returned to help Ashlee douse the flames with cold wet towels. Water splashed over the bathroom and all over the twins. The fire was extinguished by the time the firemen arrived, the sirens on the hook and ladder truck wailing.

"Amber, do me a favor," Ashlee said, catching her sister's arm after they'd led the firemen to the bathroom. "When someone asks, just say that you smelled smoke and came down here to investigate."

"But I didn't smell smoke, Ashlee. It hadn't reached the upstairs yet. I was reading in my room because I was too excited to sleep, but I had no idea there was a fire downstairs. Ashlee, if it weren't for you, the whole house could have burned down! And we might have all died of smoke inhalation before anyone could reach us." Amber's eyes grew round. "Ashlee, you knew about the fire before you'd even seen it or smelled the smoke. How did you—"

One of the firemen interrupted her to say that the blaze appeared to be completely extinguished and that they were now attempting to determine the origin of the fire.

"Please say it was you," Ashlee pleaded with her sister. "It's important to me, Amber. Please!"

The rest of the family, awakened by the sirens, noise, and confusion, gathered in the hall, which was still filled with acrid smoke. Locke, Bryce, and the two children surveyed the goings-on with bleary eyes. Alec obviously had not yet returned from Cynthia's. "What happened?" Locke asked, staring at Ashlee and Amber in their identical soaking-wet nightgowns.

"As far as we can determine, the fire started in the wastebasket of the small bathroom down the back hall from the kitchen," one of the firemen replied. "There are ashes—smells like cigar ashes—in the trash. I'd guess someone threw a smoldering cigar butt into the trash basket and eventually it burst into flames."

"Mrs. Bates!" Bryce hissed, draping his arms protectively around the shoulders of his sleepy-eyed son and daughter. "That drunken fool could have killed us all!"

"But who discovered the fire? Who called the fire department? And why are Ashlee and Amber all wet?" Locke demanded, his eyes darting from Amber to Ashlee.

"Speaking of Mrs. Bates, where is she?" Ashlee asked in an attempt to stall.

"She was taken to the hospital by the para-medics," the fireman answered.

"The hospital?" Sharon cried. "Was she burned?"

"Oh, no," the fireman assured her. "But she seemed confused and disoriented and we thought it best to send her to the hospital for observation. The effects of smoke inhalation can be—"

Bryce snorted. "Smoke inhalation, ha! The hospital tests will find the woman's blood running one hundred proof."

"I want to know who discovered the fire," Locke said firmly, his gaze fixed on Ashlee.

She nervously smoothed her hand over her wet hair, which was plastered to her head. "I feel like a drowned rat," she said, then shivered. "And a frozen one. I probably look like it too."

"You and Aunt Amber sure do look alike now," Brian piped up. "With your hair all wet and slicked back like that."

"Twin drowned rats," Sharon added.

"We keep digressing. I want to know exactly what happened," Locke said. "Now."

There was a momentary silence. Ashlee gave Amber a little nudge, her eyes pleading.

Amber took a deep breath. "Well, uh, I—um—smelled smoke." She looked from Ashlee to Locke to Bryce and the children. "So I called Ashlee and asked her to come downstairs and investigate with me."

"You called Ashlee?" echoed Bryce.

Amber nodded. "I—I saw the light on in her room and figured she must be awake. We came downstairs and—"

"There was a light on in the bedroom when you came to find Ashlee?" Locke interrupted. His eyes were riveted on Ashlee's face and hot color suffused her cheeks. Both knew what Amber would have seen had she actually come into Ashlee's bedroom. She would have discovered a pair of lovers lying in each other's arms.

"Yes, the light was on," Amber repeated eagerly. "The overhead light. Ashlee was in bed reading."

"Reading, eh?" Locke said sardonically, his gaze hard. Ashlee gulped and averted her eyes.

"Well, you were extremely quick-witted and brave, Amber." Bryce gave her an approving smile. "The firemen said you'd led Mrs. Bates to safety and extinguished the blaze before they arrived. We're all very proud of you."

"You're a hero, Aunt Amber," Brian said admiringly.

"A heroine," corrected Sharon.

Amber managed a weak smile. "I couldn't have done it without"—she linked her arm awkwardly through Ashlee's—"without my twin sister."

It should have been a beautiful moment, her twin standing by her side, acknowledging the two of them as a working team, Ashlee thought even as she eyed the stairs, longing to escape. Locke's gray-green eyes pierced and penetrated her and she fidgeted uneasily, shifting from one foot to the other while pulling at the folds of cold, wet flannel. He didn't believe Amber—the part about finding Ashlee in bed reading had killed her credibility. Next he would want to find out why his sister had felt compelled to lie. And judging by the suspicion in his eyes as he stared at her, Ashlee knew that he'd decided she was the reason.

"Let's run through the sequence of events again," Locke said. His jaw was set, his eyes now ablaze with relentless determination.

"Why?" Amber groaned. "It's late and Ashlee and I are soaked to the skin. We want to change and go to bed."

"You are sort of starting to turn blue," Sharon observed, and Ashlee could have kissed her.

"Sharon's right. Upstairs, both of you." Bryce's gaze encompassed both Amber and Ashlee. "We'll see the firemen out. You've done a splendid job tonight."

Locke extended his arm, barring the stairway. "I want to know how and why—"

Surprisingly it was Bryce who came to the sisters' rescue. "Good grief, Locke, let them alone. They've had enough for one night. I'm sure the girls will be more than willing to answer whatever questions you might have after they've had some sleep."

Ashlee and Amber exchanged glances, then hurried by Locke and up the stairs. "Amber, do you have another flannel nightgown I could borrow?" Ashlee asked breathlessly. "This is the only heavy one I have."

"Of course. Ashlee, Locke doesn't believe me. I don't know why he doesn't, but he doesn't." Amber motioned her sister to her bedroom.

"It's a perfectly logical explanation," Ashlee said. "Bryce believed it."

Amber gazed at her assessingly. "Ashlee, if you heard our conversation at the breakfast table yesterday morning, you also heard Bryce say that you fancied yourself a psychic. But it's not true, is it?"

Ashlee stared blindly ahead. What could she tell her twin? If Amber were as flatly opposed to the notion of psi ability as Locke, the future of their fragile new relationship might hinge on her answer.

"Ashlee," Amber went on, "you don't fancy yourself a psychic. You *are* one." She opened a drawer and handed Ashlee a yellow and white flannel nightgown, then removed a blue and white one for herself. "It's true, isn't it?"

"You—you don't find the whole idea preposterous? Impossible to believe?" Ashlee's voice was unsteady. Amber's acceptance of this strange sixth sense of hers was more than she'd dared to hope for.

"I don't suppose I've ever given the subject much thought, not until tonight. But tonight you knew there was a fire before you even knew where Mrs.

Bates's room was. There was no smoke on this floor and you'd never been in Mrs. Bates's bathroom, but you told me there was a fire there and . . . and there was, Ashlee."

"I could have been faking," Ashlee pointed out. "I might have been downstairs and discovered the fire and then come up to tell you, pretending that I hadn't really seen it at all."

"Part of the extortion plot, no doubt." Amber flashed a startlingly Ashlee-like grin. "Just one of the many little tricks in your scheme to bamboozle me into giving you money from my trust fund."

Ashlee dropped the nightgown and stared at her sister. "Amber, you—you believe me? You really do believe me!"

"I know you're not an extortionist or a liar. You're my twin sister and if you say you're psychic then . . ." Amber's eyes shone, lighting her thin face. "I believe you, Ashlee."

Ashlee's heart seemed to soar. "Oh, Amber, thank you." She blinked back threatening tears. "Thank you for believing in me." She enfolded her sister in an impulsive bear hug. Amber hugged her back.

"Let's dry off and go to bed," Amber said, keeping an affectionate arm around her sister. "You can sleep in the extra bed in here if you want to, Ashlee."

"I'd like that, Amber."

Amber sighed. "It's nearly five o'clock. This has been the longest—and most incredible—night of my life."

Ashlee thought of that rapturous interlude with Locke, sandwiched in between her reconciliation with Amber and the chaos of the fire. "Amen," she said wryly.

Ten

Each twin bed in Amber's room had an electric blanket, and Ashlee gratefully set the dial on high. Her hair was dry and hung loosely around her shoulders. Amber's yellow and white nightgown was a comfortable fit. She was dry and warm and she ought to be falling asleep, as Amber had done at least twenty minutes ago.

But sleep wouldn't come to Ashlee. When she closed her eyes she relived those tempestuous moments in Locke's arms and her body came sensually alive, hungering for, craving his taste and smell and touch. Ashlee flopped onto her stomach and stared into the fresh white pillowcase. Locke's face swam before her eyes, but it wasn't the face of the ardent lover who had swept her off into erotic ecstasy. It was the cold and angry face of a man who suspected that he was being duped.

Perhaps she shouldn't have asked Amber to lie about the way the fire had been discovered. Ashlee turned over again as her mind raced on. But what alternative had she had? Neither Bryce nor Locke would have believed that she'd seen the fire while lying in bed one floor away. Bryce really would have thought it all part of some con game and Locke, he would have been disbelieving and angry with her. Ashlee sighed. Exactly the way he was now.

She heard the doorknob being turned with deliberate, stealthy precision and quickly rolled onto her side, pulling the covers above her eyebrows. The door opened and Ashlee kept her eyes shut tight despite an almost overwhelming urge to peek at the intruder.

"I know you're not asleep, Ashlee." It was Locke's voice, flat and matter-of-fact.

She pulled the covers down and looked up at him. "How did you know?"

"If you'd been asleep, you wouldn't have heard me and you wouldn't have answered me. True?"

"You tricked me!" Damn! That one was as old as the Great Smokies themselves and she had fallen right into the trap. Ashlee bit her lip in vexation.

"Why aren't you sleeping?" Locke moved to stand beside the bed. He was wearing a black velour robe with dark blue and red stripes on the sleeves. It was knee-length and belted at the waist, exposing a patch of the crisp dark hair that covered his chest. Ashlee remembered the excitingly abrasive feel of that hair against the sensitive skin of her breasts and felt her nipples grow tight. She wondered if he was nude beneath his robe and guessed that he was. A flash of heat seared her and she fumbled with the electric blanket control, switching it to low.

"Guilty conscience, perhaps?" Locke asked, baiting her. "Which makes you feel guiltier, Ashlee? Your own lying? Or encouraging your twin sister to lie to her family?"

"Now, just a minute, Locke." Ashlee sat up at the same moment that he sat down on the edge of the bed. Their mutual actions brought them dangerously close and Ashlee caught her breath and swayed back, away from him.

"Amber didn't smell smoke." Locke's words were icily precise. "The smoke is only now drifting upstairs. There was none at all when that fire erupted. All six of the firemen pointed out how fortunate it was that someone happened to be downstairs to spot the blaze, because by the time the smoke had reached upstairs, the fire would have been well on its way to destroying the entire house, would have killed Mrs. Bates, and perhaps impeded the rescue of the rest of the family."

"But none of those things happened! You should be relieved, not angry," Ashlee said. "Just why are you angry, Locke?"

"As if you didn't know."

Ashlee folded her arms across her chest and leaned back against the headboard, her face impassive. Martins were also excellent at bluffing; no one in the county could beat any of them in poker. "What part of Amber's story don't you believe?"

"Try all of it. A, she didn't smell smoke. B, she didn't find the overhead light on in your room, and C, she sure as hell didn't find you reading in bed!"

Ashlee blushed despite her fiercest attempts not to. She cleared her throat and hoped she sounded sufficiently confident. "But you buy the rest of it? Calling the fire department, getting Mrs. Bates out of her room, putting out the blaze?"

"Yes, I assume that much is actually true."

"Well, that's the most important part. Why quibble over minor, meaningless details? Now, would you please leave this room so I can get some sleep?"

"No. I am not leaving this room until I hear the truth, Ashlee. It's time you learned that I will not tolerate dishonesty or deception of any kind." His tone and expression were so stern and professorial that for a moment Ashlee felt a quiver of fear. And then she reminded herself that she was not one of his students and that he had forced her into this deception he so abhorred by refusing to tolerate the truth. A quick surge of anger caused her eyes to flash. "You don't tolerate dishonesty or deception, but you do practice it, don't you, Dr. Locke Hypocrite Aames?"

"Don't try to divert the issue, Ashlee. I refuse to be sidetracked by your—" Locke interrupted himself with a frown, diverted and sidetracked despite his firm protestations. "What do you mean, I practice it?"

"She means that she knows why you took her sightseeing and spent the day with her today, Locke." The sound of Amber's thick, sleepy voice caused both Ashlee and Locke to glance swiftly at her bed. Amber was sitting up, watching them.

Locke was clearly disconcerted. "I thought you were asleep, Amber."

"I was." Amber yawned. "But neither of you were whispering, you know. Your voices rose with every word."

"I'm sorry we woke you, Amber," Ashlee said contritely. Her voice lost some of its contrition when she added, "But if you'll tell your brother to leave, we can both get some sleep."

"Leave now? Not a chance." Locke stood up, his face a hard, granite mask. "Why did I take Ashlee sightseeing today, Amber? Why did I spend the day with her?"

Amber shrugged uncomfortably. "Oh, Locke, you know why. And so does Ashlee. She overheard us talking in the kitchen, I'm ashamed to say."

"I don't seem to be able to get a straight answer from either of you." Locke's scowl deepened. "I'm still waiting to hear why Ashlee thinks I took her out today. Ashlee, maybe you'd like to answer it? And then you can tackle why you and Amber lied about the fire."

Ashlee looked up at him, towering over her like some gigantic slavemaster, and a fresh burst of anger fueled her. She hopped out of the bed, standing on the opposite side of it and imitating Locke's stance—legs aggressively apart, arms tightly folded, eyes smoldering—and glared back at him. They glowered at each other, for almost a full minute.

"Don't you two ever blink?" Amber finally said, grinning. "I feel like I'm watching a showdown between two rattlesnakes."

Ashlee and Locke ignored her. "I'm waiting for your answer, Ashlee," Locke said tightly. "I'll wait all day if I have to."

"You've seen too many John Wayne movies," Ashlee snapped. "What's next? Do you pull out your six-shooter and let me have it between the eyes?"

Locke's jaw tightened. "Oh, I'd love to let you have it. But not between the eyes, honey, and not with a six-shooter. And for your information, I've never seen a single John Wayne movie."

For a moment Ashlee was too shocked to speak. "Never seen a John Wayne movie?" she repeated incredulously. It was unheard of. The local TV station had run John Wayne movies every Sunday afternoon during her entire childhood. She and her cousins had seen some of them six and seven times each. And then she recovered herself. "Of course a *Yankee* like yourself probably likes the kind of awful movies that—"

"—shows my heroic ancestors beating the tar out of the noble Johnny Rebs," Locke finished sarcastically. "How did you guess?"

"Actually Locke seldom goes to the movies," Amber interjected quickly. "And I don't recall you ever expressing a preference for Civil War films, Locke. Your favorite has always been science fiction."

"Science, yes. Fiction, forget it," Ashlee said. "He would be in the group who tried to keep E.T. from going home. Dr. Locke Physicist Aames has no use for anything other than cold, lifeless proven facts."

"The truth," amended Locke. "Which is not what I'm getting from you, you little liar."

"Locke!" Amber gasped, clearly shocked. "Locke, this is so unlike you! I've never seen you so angry and—and cruel." Pain suddenly shadowed her eyes. "Do you think I'm a liar too?"

Ashlee looked at Amber's crestfallen face, and her twin's words seemed to echo in her ears. "He's always been my favorite brother. Locke was the one who always made time for me." Nor was Amber accustomed to raised voices and arguments, it seemed. Ashlee thought of life in the Martin homes, with anger quick to flare, to be expressed, then extinguished just as swiftly. There could be a certain exhilaration in fighting, and Ashlee had long been aware that a loss of temper didn't mean a loss of love. But perhaps Amber had yet to learn that lesson. Watching her sister, Ashlee decided that whatever her own differences with Locke, it wasn't fair to drag Amber into the fray.

"Amber, Locke doesn't think you're a liar. He loves you and cares about you. One of the reasons he's so angry with me is because I made you lie to him. Right, Locke?" She turned to him for confirmation.

He stared at her, the anger on his face fading to a puzzled frown. "Ashlee, I—"

Whatever he had been about to say was abruptly terminated by Amber's breathless denial. "But Ashlee didn't *make* me lie, Locke. I only said what I did because Bryce and the kids were there. If I were to tell Bryce what really happened . . ." She paused to glance meaningfully at Ashlee. "Ashlee, we can tell Locke the *real* truth. He'd never accuse you of anything as wild as an extortion plot."

Ashlee nervously traced the outline of her lips with her tongue. "Uh, Amber . . ."

"Locke, Ashlee is psychic," Amber forged ahead excitedly. "She really is. She knew about the fire before she actually saw it or smelled any smoke.

She even knew it was in Mrs. Bates's bathroom and she came in to get me. *I* was the one reading in bed. The rest is exactly the way I told it. You understand why I couldn't tell the whole truth to Bryce, don't you? He would never have believed it!"

"And you think I do?" Locke groaned with exasperation. "Amber, think about what you've just told me. Ashlee knew about the fire before she actually saw it or smelled the smoke? Thinking rationally now, does that make any sense at all?"

"Well . . . yes." Amber looked confused. "It makes sense because she's psychic, Locke."

"Because she's psychic," Locke muttered. "Lord, it must be in the genes."

"As you may have guessed, Bryce isn't the only skeptic I'd hoped to keep at bay," Ashlee said wearily to Amber. "Locke is just as adamantly against me."

"Not against you!" Locke said. "Against this absurd psychic nonsense! It contradicts everything I've learned, everything I know to be true. And now you've got Amber believing it too."

"I knew you'd react this way." Ashlee defiantly held Locke's gaze with her own. "That's why I asked Amber to say that she discovered the fire. But the truth—which you've insisted upon hearing—is that I saw the fire and smoke in a psychic vision while I was lying in bed." She didn't add, In your arms, after we'd made love. But she didn't have to. Locke read the unspoken in her eyes and his face reddened. At the memory? Ashlee wondered. With guilt or regret?

"Well, at least everything is out in the open now," Amber said, her tone hopeful. "Ashlee knows that I asked Locke to take her out and Locke knows who really discovered the fire. Now that neither of you is hiding anything from the other, why don't you bury the hatchet and be friends?"

"I don't think so," Ashlee said tightly. Amber still hadn't grasped the true nature of her relationship with Locke if she could suggest something as pallid as friendship between them.

"You don't think we can be friends?" Locke's face darkened.

Ashlee stared at him. Was he serious? Surely he wasn't suggesting that they be friends after . . . "No," she replied, fighting the pain that seared her. "I don't."

"Why not?" Locke challenged her. "Because you think I spent the day with you only upon Amber's suggestion? Or because I don't believe your weird, hocus-pocus stories?"

Ashlee managed a frozen, fixed smile. "I would rather be on enemy terms than pretend some sort of pseudo-friendship with you, even for Amber's sake." She started for the door. "If you'll both excuse me, I think I'll go to my room and try to get some sleep."

"Ashlee, you can stay in here, Locke is leaving now," Amber said. "I'd like you to stay," she added quietly.

"Ashlee is going to her own room. She isn't sleeping here," Locke said in a steely voice that caused Ashlee to turn around to face him. "We have a little unfinished business to attend to, don't we, Ashlee?" he continued.

She read the intent in his eyes; he made no effort to conceal it. Unfinished business! Locke Aames intended to follow her to her room . . . and to her bed!

"None that I can think of. On second thought, Amber, I think I will stay here with you." Ashlee smiled sweetly at her sister, but her blood was boiling. Did Locke actually think she would let him use her for sex when he'd made his feelings for her so brutally clear? He'd lectured her, he'd called her a liar, he'd mocked her. And now he expected her to hop into the sack with him? In the category of sheer, unmitigated gall, this man beat out all the competition!

"Ashlee, you are going to your own room," Locke said a little desperately. "I have to talk to you."

Ashlee arched her brows, giving him her most sardonic gaze. She remembered the last time he'd come to her room "to talk." "I think you've just about said it all." She purposefully lay down on the spare bed and pulled the covers around her. "And so have I." She yawned very deliberately. And then she closed her eyes.

"Ashlee!" Locke was as tense as an overwound spring. Ashlee could feel the vibrations emanating from him as he stood over her. She had no doubts that if Amber weren't present, he would be in this bed with her, on top of her, crushing her into the mattress with his solid body. She would surge upward and he would fill her, master her, make her moan and sigh with the exquisite pleasure only he could give her. And it would happen quickly, very quickly, because she was so ready for him. She was dying for him and he was just as desperate for her.

With a small gasp Ashlee pulled the covers over her head to hide the telltale flush she felt suffuse her face. It must be sleep deprivation, she consoled herself. She'd heard it was a condition with strange side effects, and now she believed it. She'd almost seduced herself into going to bed with Locke Aames—and he hadn't lifted a finger or said a word! She was extremely grateful for Amber's restraining presence. If Amber hadn't been here . . .

But Amber was very much present and pleading with her brother. "Locke, I'm tired, Ashlee's tired, and you must be tired too. Do you realize it's almost six o'clock? On normal days we'd be getting up to exercise."

"There aren't going to be any more normal days around here, Amber," Locke said grimly. "Your twin sister has seen to that."

Had Ashlee removed the covers from her face and

opened her eyes she would have seen Locke staring
down at her with painful, undisguised longing.
Amber saw and gaped at him, her eyes filling with
slowly dawning awareness. But Ashlee kept her
eyes shut and the covers over her head and what
she heard was Locke's condemnation of her. He
was sorry she had ever come to Aames. She had
disrupted all their lives and changed them for the
worse. Their days of normal, pleasant living were
over, thanks to Ashlee Rose Martin. Ashlee held
back a sob of pain.

"All right!" Locke's tone hovered between resig-
nation and exasperation. "We're all tired. I'll go to
my room and we can all get some sleep. Good
night, Amber. . . ." He paused and his voice lowered and deepened. "Good night, Ashlee."

"Good night, Locke," Amber called. "Or good
morning. Whatever." Ashlee said nothing at all.

Ashlee awakened at noon and her eyes slowly
traveled over the shelves of books that lined her sister's walls. All the books were hardcovers, unlike
her own meager library, which consisted solely of
paperbacks, right down to the cookbooks. She
reflected on that for a few sleepy moments, until
Amber emerged from the bathroom, wrapped in a
white terry robe.

"You're awake! I got up about fifteen minutes
ago and took my shower. . . ." Amber's voice
trailed off and she shrugged. She looked nervous
and uncertain, as if not at all sure how to deal with
her twin in the spare bed.

It was the morning-after-the-night-before syn-
drome, Ashlee thought wryly. The emotion-packed
events of the previous night had shoved her and
Amber into a premature intimacy that had yet to
be tested in the reality of daylight. Amber didn't
know what to expect from her sister, and Ashlee
had no intention of overwhelming her. "A shower

sounds heavenly, Amber," she said cheerfully. "Do you mind if I use your bathroom next?"

"Go right ahead. I'm going downstairs to have breakfast." Amber glanced at the clock. "Except I guess it will be lunch."

"Brunch," Ashlee compromised, and Amber nodded and smiled.

Dressed in a bright orange jumpsuit with a yellow turtleneck sweater underneath for added warmth, her hair caught up on top of her head in a loose knot, Ashlee joined Amber at the kitchen table. Amber was engrossed in the morning edition of *The Boston Globe* while munching a piece of dry whole wheat toast, the inevitable decaffeinated coffee cooling in a cup nearby.

Ashlee surveyed her sister's dark brown slacks and sweater with a suppressed sigh. Even the blouse Amber wore beneath the sweater was striped with brown. Amber glanced up and her eyes widened as she saw Ashlee's garb. "That's the . . . brightest orange I've ever seen," she said carefully. "Is that what they call Day-Glo?"

"You think it's hideous," Ashlee said dryly.

"Oh, no, not hideous! Just—just rather electrifying." Amber managed a weak smile. "I suppose you think my clothes are too drab?"

"Not drab," Ashlee hastened to assure her. "Just . . . rather somber." The twins continued to stare at each other and suddenly broke into mutual, spontaneous laughter. Ashlee felt the stilted tension dissolve and knew that the awkwardness between them had vanished forever.

"We ought to go shopping together," Amber said. "You could help me brighten up my wardrobe."

"And you could help me tone mine down," Ashlee added. "I'll never go for the monochrome look, but I should get away from wearing every color in the spectrum."

"Let's go today," Amber said eagerly. "I called the bank to tell them I wouldn't be in, but Bryce had already notified them." She sipped her coffee. "Ashlee, do you know that this is the first time I've ever taken a day off work? Even when I've been sick I've gone in. I feel so . . . so free." Her face was alight with animation, her resemblance to Ashlee unmistakable. "Do you want to go shopping today, Ashlee? Or perhaps you'd rather do more sightseeing?"

"Actually"—Ashlee sank into the kitchen chair—"I want to go home, Amber."

"Home? To North Carolina?"

Suddenly the urge to leave Aames was as strong as the urge to go there had been. Ashlee thought of all she had left behind and made her decision with her customary impetuosity. "Come with me, Amber. We can leave today, as soon as we've packed."

"Leave today?" parroted Amber. "But I thought you were going to stay until the weekend, Ashlee. And after last night, I—I supposed you might stay . . . even longer."

"Amber, I've found you, there's no need for me to stay here." Ashlee's thoughts drifted to Locke, and her heart contracted with pain. Her need to leave increased. She was in love with a man who desired her sexually, but personally despised her. And one more clairvoyant episode would probably kill even his desire for her. To Locke Aames her gift of ESP was a definite turnoff. And what would happen then? She'd seen his utter indifference to Cynthia when he'd decided that she held no interest for him. To be forced to endure *that*, his disinterest and disregard . . . Ashlee gave herself a mental shake. She simply couldn't—and she didn't have to.

"Amber, you don't have to make any final, binding decisions about the future. Just put everything here on hold and come away with me and enjoy yourself for a while."

"But what about Locke, Ashlee?"

Ashlee blanched. "What about him?"

"I know I'm not very well versed in male-female relationships, but last night I began to think that . . . I had the impression that . . ." Amber sighed. "Ashlee, I've never seen my brother look at a woman—look at anything—the way he looked at you."

"With undisguised contempt, you mean? With unadulterated loathing?"

"My experience might be limited, but I'm not blind, Ashlee. Believe me, he wasn't looking at you with loathing or contempt."

"Disgust, perhaps?"

"Ashlee, Locke looked as if he wanted to pick you up and carry you off and never let you go."

"You've been reading too many romance novels, Amber."

"Why, I've never read one in my life!" Amber looked taken aback. "Do you . . . think I should start?"

"I think you should come home with me. Please, Amber!"

"You're going to leave today whether I come with you or not," Amber said thoughtfully. "Aren't you, Ashlee?"

"I have to, Amber. Please don't think I'm issuing any ultimatums though. If you can't come with me now, you're welcome to visit me anytime. Anytime at all."

A slow smile tilted the corners of Amber's mouth. "I'll do it, Ashlee. It's about time I made a move that hasn't been planned for months in advance."

Ashlee hugged her. "I'll start packing."

"I have a few phone calls to make," Amber said, returning the hug. "Then I'll pack too."

The monotony of the interstate highway didn't end when Ashlee's little orange Rabbit crossed the Massachusetts stateline and entered Connecticut.

Amber turned to glance behind her, then stared ahead in pensive silence. "Are you sorry you came, Amber?" Ashlee asked softly. It didn't require any special insight to perceive Amber's apprehensive tension.

"No! No, I'm not sorry," Amber hastened to assure her. "It's just that . . . I've never done anything quite like this before." She grimaced wryly. "And you don't know the half of it."

"Well, I'm so happy that you're with me." Ashlee reached over to give her sister's hand an impulsive squeeze. "More than I can ever say, Amber." It had been difficult enough to leave Locke behind. Had Amber not come along with her, Ashlee wondered if she would have had the courage to go. And she had to go. It would have hurt too much to stay.

"Ashlee, I looked over our original birth certificates," Amber said. She glanced at the sideview mirror, then turned to face Ashlee. "Do you realize our mother, our biological mother," she corrected herself hastily, "Caroline Rose Sheppard, was only nineteen years old when she had us? She would be forty-four today. That's not much older than Bryce."

"She was almost six years younger than we are now when we were born," Ashlee said. "It's hard to imagine, isn't it? Being pregnant with twins at nineteen?"

"Being pregnant with twins at nineteen and unmarried," Amber added succinctly. "I wonder who the father was? The birth certificate lists him as John Doe. A more obvious pseudonym you'll never find."

"Not *the* father, Amber, *our* father. I wonder why she, Caroline, didn't put down his real name?" Ashlee's eyes held a dreamy, faraway look. "Maybe they were passionately in love but tragic circumstances kept them apart." She warmed to the notion. "Maybe he was the sole support of a large, poor family and though he loved Caroline, he knew he could never marry her because he had to marry for money so his little sister could have the heart operation or kidney transplant she so desperately needed. His poor widowed mother and the rest of the children—"

"What bathos!" Amber rolled her eyes. "More than likely John Doe was a married man and Caroline Sheppard was stupid enough to fool around with him without taking the proper precautions."

"Married man?"

"Kidney transplant?"

The twins began to laugh. "Well, whoever they were," Ashlee said, "I'm glad they had us. Do you want to search for them, Amber? I was in touch with an adoption search and support group when I started looking for you. We could join again and—"

"Ask me again in about five years," Amber interrupted dryly. "I'm not up to the tragic, dramatic romance of John and Caroline at this point in time."

"Oh, Amber, I'm so glad I found you!" Ashlee exclaimed, laughing along with her twin.

"Me, too, Ashlee. I think we're going to be very good for each other." Amber turned to glance at the traffic behind them. "I've already begun to do things I wouldn't have dreamed of doing before I met you."

It was a bittersweet moment for Ashlee. She may not have the man she loved, but she had her twin sister's love, and after their long separation that was no mere consolation prize. Amber was in her life even if Locke wasn't and Ashlee would have to build on that. As Gran said, "Happiness isn't having what you want, it's wanting what you have." Ashlee blinked back a sudden surge of tears. She was unaware that Amber had been observing her until her sister patted her arm in a consoling gesture.

"It's going to be all right, Ashlee." Amber's velvet brown eyes glowed with promise.

"Yes." Ashlee sniffled, determined not to break down. "We have each other, Amber."

By six o'clock it was as dark as midnight and the headlights of the other cars on the highway were beginning to blur. Ashlee rubbed her eyes, and stifled a yawn.

"You're tired," Amber said. "Why don't we find a motel and stop for the night, Ashlee? We're already in New Jersey and there's no need to push ourselves on this drive. I saw a sign for a motel at the next exit."

"Sounds good to me," Ashlee agreed.

"Don't forget to signal that you're turning off at the exit." Amber glanced at the stream of cars behind them and Ashlee smiled indulgently at her. "You really worry about being rear-ended on the road, don't you, Amber? You've reminded me to signal and checked the cars in back of us every time I've had to make a turn."

Amber gnawed at her thumbnail. "One of my many little hang-ups, I guess."

The motel room was surprisingly spacious. Ashlee heaved a tired sigh and flopped down on one of the two queen-sized beds. "I'm glad we stopped. Staying up all night last night and sleeping all morning has wrecked my internal time clock."

"Mine too," Amber said absently. She was pacing the room, chewing anxiously on her thumbnail. "Ashlee, would you mind if I went to the lobby? I—I saw, um, a c-candy machine there and—and—"

Ashlee laughed at her twin's discomfiture. "Amber, I'm not going to give you a lecture on the poisonous effects of sugar in the bloodstream. Go ahead, indulge yourself! And bring back a Hershey bar for me." She was still smiling after Amber had left the room. It was going to be fun to watch her sister loosen up and shed all the restrictive prohibitions she had imposed upon herself.

Ashlee sat up to switch on the color TV set and suddenly all traces of her smile vanished. In her mind's eye she saw Amber enter the motel lobby and walk straight into the arms of her brother Locke. Ashlee uttered a hoarse cry of protest. Locke Aames? Here? No, it wasn't possible! She must be hallucinating! Unless . . .

She drew a sharp breath and gulped. Unless he'd followed them here. Amber had been closeted in her bedroom for over an hour this afternoon, making phone calls and packing, she'd said. Had she notified Locke of their departure? Was *he* the reason Amber had continually checked the traffic behind them? And insisted that Ashlee give clear, *easy-to-follow* traffic signals?

Ashlee opened the door just as Locke was preparing to knock. Amber was nowhere in sight. The two of them stared at each other. "May I come in?" Locke asked at last.

Ashlee shrugged and stepped inside. "Where's Amber?"

"Having dinner in the motel dining room. Don't be angry with her, Ashlee." Locke entered the room and swung the door shut behind him. "You knew I was here. You opened the door before I knocked."

Ashlee only nodded, not trusting herself to speak.

"Did you know I've been following you since you left Aames?" His mouth twisted into a rueful grin. "I tried to be so careful. I even borrowed Alec's car so as to not arouse your—er—suspicions."

"You were successful. I didn't know you were here until I saw you greet Amber in the lobby." Her eyes flashed with sudden defiance. "The lobby is on the opposite side of the building and I saw you from this room, with the door shut and the curtains drawn."

Locke didn't rise to the bait. He merely nodded as

he removed his gray winter coat. "Would you mind telling me why we're here, Ashlee?" He was wearing a dark blue vested suit with a white shirt and a blue and silver striped tie. Ashlee's eyes drank in the sight of him. He looked elegantly, powerfully masculine. "Amber called me out of a luncheon honoring two German biophysicists. I had to plead a family emergency and leave immediately."

"But why?" Ashlee asked, her eyes wide with shock. He'd left a career function to come chasing after her and Amber?

"You tell me, Ashlee." She watched in mesmerized fascination as he removed his suit coat, vest, and tie. When he'd taken off his cuff links and rolled the sleeves of his shirt to his elbows, she began to back slowly toward the door. "You told me that you weren't the type who ran from problems," he said as he unfastened the top two buttons of his shirt. "You faced them, you said."

"There's a difference between running from a problem and removing oneself from an impossible situation," Ashlee retorted, continuing her steady backward pace. "Anyway, I—I wanted to go home."

"I thought a wife's home was with her husband." Locke advanced toward her, his voice maddeningly calm. "Another one of our demented Yankee concepts, no doubt."

Ashlee backed into the door with a thud and stared at him, incredulous.

"You'll go through the door if you try to back up any farther," Locke said. He was directly in front of her now, and he braced his hands against the door on either side of her, effectively trapping her. Ashlee stared pointedly at his shoes, trying to block out the overwhelming effects of his nearness.

"You've known from the first day we met that you were going to marry me," he continued in those killingly rational tones. "It occurred to me during my damnable eight o'clock sophomore physics class. While the students slaved over their assignment I found myself reliving the sweet moments of our first quarrel. You glared at me and screamed like a banshee that you wouldn't marry me. It made no sense at the time, but in retrospect . . ." He laughed huskily and lowered his head to caress the satiny softness of her neck with his lips. Ashlee felt a stab of primitive desire deep inside her. "Poor little Ashlee," Locke murmured, "railing against her fate. But it's hopeless, sweetheart. You belong to me and you're going to marry me. I think I've known that since the *second* day we met and without benefit of the—er—paranormal." He arched against her, letting her feel the full weight of his burgeoning arousal.

"You're crazy," Ashlee moaned, placing her hands against his chest to push him away. But her feeble attempts were ineffective against his determined strength.

"That's what I told mysef." Locke was nibbling on her neck, his tongue and teeth and warm breath making her his erotic captive. Ashlee's hands stopped pushing and her fingers slipped inside his starched shirt to tangle in the mat of chest hair. "Crazy," she repeated breathlessly, lovingly.

"And that's just what Bryce called me when he found me in the garden with a crowbar at six-fifteen this morning." Locke moved his hips against her in a sensuous, rhythmic stimulation that took her breath away. "There is an old sundial with a marble inlay in the garden, Ashlee." His hands moved to her waist to position her snugly against his body. "You know what I found when I pried the marble top off with the crowbar, don't you, love?"

Ashlee knew. "Your uncle's golden guineas."

"Reach inside my pocket," Locke said, taking her hand and guiding it to the deep pocket of his trousers. She felt the solid muscles of his thigh beneath her fingers as she withdrew the coins. She studied them as they lay in her palm. They were the coins she had seen that night.

"My share of the wealth," Locke said. "Bryce wasn't about to allow a lunatic to handle the others'. I'm sure he has them safely stashed away in a bank vault by now. But these are yours, Ashlee."

"Mine?" Ashlee tried to draw back, but Locke's hold merely tightened, chaining her to him. "Locke, I can't keep these coins. They're valuable, part of your inheritance."

"My son's inheritance," corrected Locke. "Or daughter's." His gray-green eyes were ablaze with a passion that melted all her resistance. "Which is it going to be, darling? A son or a daughter?"

Her whole body burned with the knowledge she had somehow just acquired. "Both," she whispered.

"One of each." Locke's lips hovered above hers. "Two beautiful children."

"No, my darling." Ashlee smiled and shook her head. "Five."

"What? Five?" Locke dropped his arms and backed away with the swiftness of one trying to escape from a lighted stick of dynamite. "You're making that up!" he accused.

"No, I'm not. There's a set of twins and a—a couple of passionate accidents!" Ashlee threw up her hands in angry despair. "Oh, what's the use? Go back to Aames, Locke. It'll never work between us. You can't accept me for what I am. I'd always have to lie to you and you wouldn't like that either. We'd end up fighting all the time. It would be an awful, impossible existence!"

"No!" Locke took a step toward her, his face pale. "It isn't going to be like that, Ashlee. Darling, I love you."

"No, you don't. I turn you on. You want to *make* love to me, but you don't love me."

"I assure you that I know the difference between the two, Ashlee. And I do love you. I want to marry you and"—he smiled bravely—"have five children with you." He held open his arms to her. "Come here, sweetheart. Let me hold you."

Ashlee stood stock-still. "And what about the nasty little issue of my—my clairvoyance? I'm almost afraid to use the word around you, Locke. You can't accept it, you don't believe in it, and you hate the whole idea of it. It will always stand between us."

"Nothing is going to stand between us," Locke said fiercely. "I'm beginning to come to grips with it, Ashlee. With your clairvoyance," he amended deliberately. "I looked for the coins and I really wasn't surprised when I found them. And last night I suspected how the fire was really discovered. I think I knew you'd seen it in one of those visions of yours. I also knew that you felt you couldn't tell me, that you felt you had to lie to me."

"You were so angry with me," Ashlee whispered.

"I was angry with myself, Ashlee. Such things weren't supposed to happen in my precise, logical world. I've seldom come up against anything that I couldn't understand and fit into clear, concise principles."

"And then you met me. Poor Locke." Ashlee reached out to touch his cheek. "My life has been imprecise, inconcise, unclear, and illogical all the way."

"And I adore you." Locke took her hand in his and slowly pulled her to him. "Don't doom me to the sterile existence I was enduring before I met you, Ashlee. You've brought passion and wonder and joy into my life. With you I feel totally alive. With you I've reached the full measure of myself as a man."

His words touched her heart. Ashlee couldn't resist him. Somehow, in some way, they would overcome all the obstacles. Maybe they'd already partially done so tonight. She moved into his arms and hugged him, resting her head against his chest. "I love you so, Locke."

"And you'll marry me?"

"Yes."

"And be my friend?"

"Of course."

"Last night you said you couldn't be my friend," he reminded her. "And it hurt like hell, sweetheart."

"I want to be everything to you, Locke." Ashlee lifted her head and gazed up at him adoringly. "Your wife, your friend, your lover. Everything a woman can be to a man. I'll even be a Yankee for you."

"We won't live with my family," Locke said firmly. "I want to be alone with you, at least until all those future Aameses begin to arrive. We'll buy a house—a big one—of our own in Cambridge or Boston, wherever you want."

He suddenly looked doubtful. "That is, if you don't mind moving here. I could probably work at some other university, but M.I.T.—"

Ashlee pressed a finger against his lips. "I'm adaptable. I could even get used to your Yankee winters—in about fifty years. But would you mind if I kept working, maybe even opened a new shop? I love my work, Locke, and . . ."

"Of course I don't mind," he said. "Your work is just as important as mine, and think of the money we'll save on toys," he added, teasing.

Ashlee grinned. "And we'll have a television set and *real* food and—"

Locke silenced her with a hard, swift kiss. A magical kiss, Ashlee thought dreamily, one of passion and tenderness, caring and commitment. A promise of what their life together would hold.

"I have something for you, love," Locke murmured softly against her mouth. "I'd planned to give it to you tonight after I'd—" He broke off at the sight of Ashlee's face, alight with excited anticipation. "You know!" he gasped. "You know, don't you?"

"Know about what?" Ashlee asked innocently.

"Admit it, Ashlee. You know I have a ring for you."

"A sapphire surrounded by diamonds? The most beautiful ring I've ever seen? In a dark blue velvet-lined box in the inside pocket of your gray coat? Is that for me?"

Locke retrieved the small box from his coat and opened it. The ring Ashlee had described was resting in a bed of bright blue velvet. "Incredible!" He shook his head, looking a little dazed. "I'm beginning to accept the existence of psi, honey, but I don't think I'll ever get used to it. Or understand it."

"Does it matter, Locke?" Ashlee asked quietly.

He slipped the ring on her finger. "No, I guess it really doesn't."

"Then you won't mind my telling you that at this very moment Amber's at the registration desk getting a room for herself for tonight?"

His eyes danced with laughter as he pulled Ashlee into a tight embrace. "No, sweetheart, I don't think I mind one bit."

"Amber is going to be so happy, Locke."

He chuckled. "Yet another vision?"

She drew back. "Are you *sure* it doesn't bother you?"

Locke hugged her enthusiastically. "The world is full of mysteries that defy rational explanation. Here's one example. How did a rather rigid, compulsive, Yankee scientific stiff manage to get engaged to a beautiful, warm, and loving angel from the South?"

"You're just fishing for compliments, Locke Aames. You want me to tell you how fantastically handsome, sexy, and dynamic you are."

"The woman is telepathic too."

Ashlee caught his hand and pulled him to the bed. "First I'll tell you," she said lovingly. "Then I'll show you."

THE EDITOR'S CORNER

Last month I told you about the long novels coming from LOVESWEPT authors in the Bantam Books' general list. And now this month you get a special treat: an excerpt from Sandra Brown's riveting historical romance, **SUNSET EMBRACE**. It's right in the back of this book and I'm sure the brief glimpse into the lives of Lydia and Ross will intrigue you so much that you'll want to ask your bookseller to hold a copy of **SUNSET EMBRACE** for you. It's due on the racks early next month.

Sandra really packs a double whammy for romance readers next month because you can also look forward to a LOVESWEPT from her! And "double whammy" is not only apt for the long historical plus short contemporary publication, but as a description of her LOVESWEPT #79. In **THURSDAY'S CHILD** heroine Allison is a twin. And she is persuaded to "pull a switch" by her sister Ann who couldn't be more different from Allison if she'd been born to other parents. And then along comes Spencer Raft—one of those extraordinarily dashing and sensual men that Sandra dreams up—and scientist Allison is the beneficiary of some very special "experimental" help from Spencer. **THURSDAY'S CHILD** is so humorous and has such wonderful love scenes that you definitely will *not* want to miss it!

With only two romances published (**BREAKING ALL THE RULES**, LOVESWEPT #61 and **CHARADE**, LOVESWEPT #74), Joan Elliott Pickart has certainly found her place in readers' hearts. Joan and all of us

(continued)

here are very grateful for your letters praising those books. Well, here's cause for rejoicing about her romances again: **THE FINISHING TOUCH**, LOVESWEPT #80. Paige Cunningham is one of the most heartwarming of heroines. I was routing for her from first word until last as she and Kellen Davis fell in love and confronted their problems. Paige is an interior decorator and Kellen is an actor. She is working on his new home and there are some truly comic scenes as Kellen traipses along to help her shop for furnishings. And there is a love scene of such compassion and tenderness between them that I am positive you will never forget **THE FINISHING TOUCH**.

I found Joan Bramsch's offering for next month—**THE LIGHT SIDE**, LOVESWEPT #81—a marvelous romance ... spritely, downright funny and terribly touching. Savvy Alexander entertains at children's parties dressed as a clown. Balloons are her "signature," and when she meets hero Sky Brady she's in an elevator (stuck!) that's crammed with balloons. Sky comes to the rescue, but very soon decides he needs rescuing—emotionally—from one dynamite little lady clown. But there are major obstacles to overcome before these two wonderful folks can find true, committed love. **THE LIGHT SIDE** has its serious side too and will appeal to all your emotions.

Last—but never, never least—Iris Johansen is back! Iris interrupted work on her second long novel for Bantam to write two LOVESWEPTS. First, you'll delight in **WHITE SATIN**, LOVESWEPT #82, in which Iris portrays the trials and tribulations of Dany Alexander. Dany is reaching to win the gold in Olympic ice skating competition while trying desperately to achieve happiness with her mentor Anthony Malik. This is a love story in typical "Iris Johansen tradition"—glowingly emotional, fast-paced, and as deliciously sensual as that title, **WHITE SATIN.** Now, you know our lovably tricky Iris, so you'd better read carefully if you want to discover which of the secondary characters in **WHITE SATIN** will be the hero of her LOVESWEPT #86, coming month after next, **BLUE VELVET.**

May your New Year be filled with all the best things in life—the company of good friends and family, peace and prosperity, and, of course, love.

Warm wishes for a wonderful 1985 from all of us at LOVESWEPT,

Carolyn Nichols

Carolyn Nichols
   Editor
LOVESWEPT
Bantam Books, Inc.
666 Fifth Avenue
New York, NY 10103

Read this special preview of

Sunset Embrace

by Sandra Brown

Coming from Bantam Books this January

They were two untamed outcasts on a Texas-bound wagon train, two passionate travelers, united by need, threatened by pasts they could not outrun. . . .

Lydia Russell—*voluptuous and russet-haired, fleeing from a secret shame, vowing that never again would a man, any man, overpower her. . . .*

Ross Coleman—*dark, brooding, and iron-willed, with the shadow of a lawless past in his piercing eyes, sworn to resist the temptation of his wanton longings. . . .*

Fate threw them together on the same wild road, where they fought the breathtaking desire blazing between them, while the shadows of their enemies grew longer. As the wagon train rolled west, the danger of them drew ever closer, until a showdown with their pursuers was inevitable. Before it was over, Lydia and Ross would face death . . . the truth about each other . . . and the astonishing strength of their love. . . .

She liked the way his hair fell over his forehead. His head was bent over as he cleaned his guns. The rifle, already oiled and gleaming, was propped against the side of the wagon. Now he was working on a pistol. Lydia knew nothing of guns, but this particular one frightened her. Its steel barrel was long and slender, cold and lethal. Ross brought it up near his face and peered down the barrel, blowing on it gently. Then he concentrated on rubbing it again with a soft cloth.

Their first day of marriage had passed uneventfully. The weather was still gloomy, but it wasn't raining as steadily or as hard as it had been. Nevertheless, it was damp and cool and Lydia had spent most of the day in the wagon. Ross had gotten up early, while it was still dark, and had shuffled through trunks and boxes. He seemed intent on the task, and she had pretended to sleep, not daring to ask what he was doing. When she did get up and began to move about the wagon she noticed that everything that had belonged to Victoria was gone. She didn't know what Ross had done with Victoria's things, but there was nothing of hers left in the wagon.

Lydia watched him now as he unconsciously pushed back his hair with raking fingers. His hair was always clean and glossy, even when his hat had mashed it down. It was getting long over his neck and ears. Lydia thought the black strands might feel very good against her fingers if she ever had occasion to touch them, which she couldn't imagine having the nerve to do even if he would allow it. She doubted he would. He treated her politely, but never commenced a conversation, and certainly never touched her.

"Tell me about your place in Texas," she said softly, bringing his green eyes away from the pistol to meet hers in the glow of the single lantern. She was holding the baby, rocking him gently, although he had finished nursing for the night and was already sleeping. They were killing the minutes until it was time to go to bed.

"I don't know much about it yet," he said, turning his attention back to his project. He briefly told her the same story about John Sachs that he had told Bubba. "He sent for the deed and, when it came back in the mail, there was a surveyor's description attached to it."

His enthusiasm for the property overrode his restraint and the words poured out. "It sounds beautiful. Rolling pastureland. Plenty of water. There's a branch of the Sabine River that flows through a part of it. The report said it has two wooded areas with oak, elm, pecan, cottonwoods near the river, pine, dogwood—"

"I love dogwood trees in the springtime when they bloom," Lydia chimed in excitedly.

Ross found himself smiling with her, until he realized he was doing it and quickly ducked his head again. "First thing I'll have to do is build a corral for the horses and a lean-to for us." The word had fallen naturally from his lips. Us. He glanced at her furtively, but she was stroking Lee's head and watched the dark baby hair fall back into its swirls after it was disturbed. Lee's head was pillowed on her breasts. For an instant Ross thought of his own head there, her touching his hair that way with that loving expression on her face.

He shifted uncomfortably on his stool. "Then, before winter, I'll have to build a cabin. It won't be fancy," he said with more force than necessary, like he was warning her not to expect anything special from him.

She looked at him with unspoken reproach. "It'll be fine, whatever it is."

He rubbed the gun barrel more aggressively. "Next spring I hope all the mares foal. That'll be my start. And who knows, maybe I can sell timber off the land to make some extra money, or put Lucky out to stud."

"I'm sure you'll make a success of it."

He wished she wouldn't be so damned optimistic. It was contagious. He could feel his heart accelerating over the unlimited prospects of a place of his own with heavy woods and fertile soil, and a prize string of horses. And he wouldn't have to be looking over his shoulder all the time either. He had never been in Texas. There wouldn't be as much threat of someone recognizing him.

Lost in his memories, he snapped the barrel back into place, spun the loaded six-bullet chamber, and twirled the pistol on his index finger with uncanny talent before taking aim on an imaginary target.

Lydia stared at him with fascination. When it occurred to Ross what he had done out of reflex, he jerked his head around to see if she had noticed. Her dark amber eyes were wide with incredulity. He shoved the pistol into its holster as if to deny that it existed.

She licked her lips nervously. "How . . . how far is your land from Jefferson?"

"About a day's ride by wagon. Half a day on horseback. As near as I can figure it on the map."

"What will we do when we get to Jefferson?"

She had listened to the others in the train enough to know that Jefferson was the second largest city in Texas. It was an inland port in the northeastern corner of the state that was connected to the Red River via Cypress Creek and Caddo Lake. The Red flowed into the Mississippi in Louisiana. Jefferson was a commercial center with paddle-wheelers bringing supplies from the east and New Orleans in exchange for taking cotton down to the markets in that city. For settlers moving into the state, it was a stopping-off place where they purchased wagons and household goods before continuing their trek westward.

"We won't have any trouble selling the wagon. I hear there's a waiting list for them. Folks are camped for miles around just waiting for more wagons to be built. I'll buy a flatbed before we continue on."

Lydia had been listening, but her mind was elsewhere. "Would you like me to trim your hair?"

"What?" His head came up like a spring mechanism was operating it.

Lydia swallowed her caution. "Your hair. It keeps falling over your eyes. Would you like me to cut it for you?"

He didn't think that was a good idea. Damn. He *knew* that wasn't a good idea. Still, he couldn't leave the idea alone. "You've got your hands full," he mumbled, nodding toward Lee.

She laughed. "I'm spoiling him rotten. I should

have put him in his bed long ago." She turned to do just that, tucking the baby in a light blanket to keep the damp air off him.

She had on one of the shirtwaists and skirts he had financed the day before. He wasn't going to let it be said that Ross Coleman wouldn't take care of his wife, any more than he was going to let it be said that he was sleeping outside his own wagon when he had a new wife sleeping inside. It was hell on him and he didn't know how he was going to survive many more nights like the sleepless one he had spent last night. But his pride had to be served. After a suitable time when suspicions would no longer be aroused, he would start sleeping outside. Many of the men did, giving up the wagons to their wives and children.

She liked those new clothes. She had folded and refolded them about ten times throughout the day. Ross couldn't decide if she was a woman accustomed to having fine clothes who had fallen on bad times, or a woman who had never possessed any clothes so fine. When it came right down to it, he didn't know anything about her. But then, she didn't know about him either, nor did anyone else.

All he knew of her was that a man had touched her, kissed her, known her intimately. And the more Ross thought about that, the more it drove him crazy. Who was the man and where was he now? Every time Ross looked at her, he could imagine that man lying on her, kissing her mouth, her breasts, burying his hands in her hair, fitting his body deep into hers. What disturbed him most was that the image had begun to wear his face.

"Do you have any scissors?"

Ross nodded, knowing he was jumping from the frying pan into the fire and condemning himself to another night of sleepless misery. He wanted badly to hate her. He also wanted badly to bed her.

He resumed his seat on the stool after he had given her the scissors. She draped a towel around his neck and told him to hold it together with one hand. Then she stood away from him, tilting her head first to one side then the other as she studied him.

When she lifted the first lock of his hair, he caught her wrist with his free hand. "You aren't going to butcher me, are you? Do you know what you're doing?"

"Sure," she said, teasing laughter shining like a sunbeam in her eyes. "Who do you think cuts *my* hair?" His face drained of color and took on a sickly expression. She burst out laughing. "Scared you, didn't I?" She shook off his hand and made the first snip with the scissors. "I don't think you'll be too mutilated." She stepped behind him to work on the back side first.

His hair felt as good coiling over her fingers as she had thought it would. It was course and thick, yet silky. She played with it more than she actually cut, hoping to prolong the pleasure. They chatted inconsequentially about Lee, about the various members of the train, and laughed over Luke Langston's latest mischievous antic.

The dark strands fell to his shoulders and then drifted to the floor of the wagon as she deftly maneuvered the scissors around his head. It was an effort to keep his voice steady when her breasts pressed into his back as she leaned forward or glanced his arm as she moved from one spot to another. Once a clump of hair fell onto his ear. Lydia bent at the waist and blew on it gently. Ross's arm shot up and all but knocked her to the floor.

"What are you doing?" Her warm breath on his skin had sent shafts of desire firing through him like cannonballs. His hand all but made a garrote out of the towel around his neck. The other hand balled into a tight fist where it rested on the top of his thigh.

She was stunned. "I . . . I was . . . what? What did I do?"

"Nothing," he growled. "Just hurry the hell up and get done with this."

Her spirits sank. They had been having such an easy time. She had acutally begun to hope that he might come to like her. She moved around to his front, hoping to rectify whatever she had done to startle him so, but he had become even more still and tense.

Ross had decided that if she were to trim his hair, it was necessary for her fingers to be sliding through it. He had even decided that it was necessary for her to lay her hand along his cheek to turn his head. He had decided that this was going to feel good no matter how much he didn't want it to and that he might just as well sit back and enjoy her attention.

But when he had felt her breath, heavy and warm and fragrant, whispering around his ear, it had all the impact of a strike of lightning. The bolt went straight from his head to his loins and ignited them.

If that weren't bad enough, now she was standing in front of him between his knees—it had been only natural to open them so she could move closer and not have to reach so far. Her breasts were directly in his line of vision and looked as tempting as ripe peaches waiting to be picked. God, but didn't she know what she was doing? Couldn't she tell by the fine sheen of sweat on his face that she was driving him slowly crazy. Each time she moved, he was tantalized by her scent, by the supple grace of her limbs, by the rustling of the clothes against her body which hinted at mysteries worth discovering.

"I'm almost done," she said when he shifted restlessly on the stool. Her knees had come dangerously close to his vulnerable crotch.

Oh, God, no! She leaned down closer to trim the hair on the crown of his head. Raising her arms higher, her breasts were lifted as well. If he inclined forward a fraction of an inch, he would nuzzle her with his nose and chin and mouth, bury his face in the lushness and breathe her, imbibe her. His lips, with searching lovebites, would find her nipple.

He hated himself. He plowed through his memory, trying to recall a time when Victoria had been such a temptation to him, or a time when he had felt free to put his hands over her breasts for the sheer pleasure of holding them. He couldn't. Had there ever been such a time?

No. Victoria hadn't been the kind of woman who deliberately lured a man, reducing him to an animal. Every time Ross made love to Victoria it had been with reverence and an attitude of worship. He had entered her body as one walks into a church, a little ashamed for what he was, apologetic because he wasn't worthy, a supplicant for mercy, contrite that such a temple was defiled by his presence.

There was nothing spiritual in what he was feeling now. He was consumed by undiluted carnality. Lydia was a woman who inspired that in a man, who had probably inspired it as a profession, despite her denials. She was trying to work the tricks of her trade on him by looking and acting as innocent as a virgin bride.

Well, by God, it wasn't going to work!

"Your moustache needs trimming too."

"What?" he asked stupidly, by now totally disoriented. He saw nothing but the feminine form before him, heard nothing but the pounding of his own pulse.

"Your moustache. Be very still." Bending to the task, she carefully clipped away a few longish hairs in his moustache, working her mouth in the way she wanted his to go.

Had he been looking at her comical, mobile mouth, it might have made him laugh. Instead he had lowered his eyes to trace the arch of her throat. The skin of it looked creamy at the base before it melded into the more velvety texture of her chest that disappeared into the top of her shirtwaist. Did she smell more like honeysuckle or magnolia blossoms?

Every sensory receptor in his body went off like a fire bell when she lightly touched his moustache, brushing his lips free of the clipped hairs with her fingertips. First to one side, then the other, her finger glided over his mouth. The choice was his. He could either stop her, or he could explode.

He pushed her hands away and said gruffly, "That's enough."

"But there's one—"

"Dammit, I said that's enough," he shouted, whipping the towel from around his neck and flinging it to the floor as he came off the stool. "Clean this mess up."

Lydia was at first taken off guard by his rudeness and his curt order, but anger soon overcame astonishment. She grabbed his hand and slapped the scissors into his palm with a resounding whack. "You clean it up. It's your hair. And haven't you ever heard the words 'thank you' before?"

With that she spun away from him and, after having taken off her skirt and shirtwaist and carefully folding them, crawled into her pallet, giving him her back as she pulled the covers over her shoulders.

He stood watching her in speechless fury before turning away to find the broom.

#1 HEAVEN'S PRICE
By Sandra Brown
Blair Simpson had enclosed herself in the fortress of her dancing, but Sean Garrett was determined to love her anyway. In his arms she came to understand the emotions behind her dancing. But could she afford the high price of love?

#2 SURRENDER
By Helen Mittermeyer
Derry had been pirated from the church by her ex-husband, from under the nose of the man she was to marry. She remembered every detail that had driven them apart—and the passion that had drawn her to him. The unresolved problems between them grew . . . but their desire swept them toward surrender.

#3 THE JOINING STONE
By Noelle Berry McCue
Anger and desire warred within her, but Tara Burns was determined not to let Damon Mallory know her feelings. When he'd walked out of their marriage, she'd been hurt.

Damon had violated a sacred trust, yet her passion for him was as breathtaking as the Grand Canyon.

#4 SILVER MIRACLES
By Fayrene Preston
Silver-haired Chase Colfax stood in the Texas moonlight, then took Trinity Ann Warrenton into his arms. Overcome by her own needs, yet determined to have him on her own terms, she struggled to keep from losing herself in his passion.

#5 MATCHING WITS
By Carla Neggers
From the moment they met, Ryan Davis tried to outmaneuver Abigail Lawrence. She'd met her match in the Back Bay businessman. And Ryan knew the Boston lawyer was more woman than any he'd ever encountered. Only if they vanquished their need to best the other could their love triumph.

#6 A LOVE FOR ALL TIME
By Dorothy Garlock
A car crash had left its marks on Casey Farrow's beauty. So what were Dan

Murdock's motives for pursuing her? Guilt? Pity? Casey had to choose. She could live with doubt and fear . . . or learn a lesson in love.

#7 A TRYST WITH MR. LINCOLN?
By Billie Green
When Jiggs O'Malley awakened in a strange hotel room, all she saw were the laughing eyes of stranger Matt Brady . . . all she heard were his teasing taunts about their "night together" . . . and all she remembered was nothing! They evaded the passions that intoxicated them until . . . there was nowhere to flee but into each other's arms.

#8 TEMPTATION'S STING
By Helen Conrad
Taylor Winfield likened Rachel Davidson to a Conus shell, contradictory and impenetrable. Rachel battled for independence, torn by her need for Taylor's embraces and her impassioned desire to be her own woman. Could they both succumb to the temptation of the tropi-

cal paradise and still be true to their hearts?

#9 DECEMBER 32nd . . . AND ALWAYS
By Marie Michael
Blaise Hamilton made her feel like the most desirable woman on earth. Pat opened herself to emotions she thought she'd buried with her late husband. Together they were unbeatable as they worked to build the jet of her late husband's dreams. Time seemed to be running out and yet—would ALWAYS be long enough?

#10 HARD DRIVIN' MAN
By Nancy Carlson
Sabrina sensed Jacy in hot pursuit, as she maneuvered her truck around the racetrack, and recalled his arms clasping her to him. Was he only using her feelings so he could take over her trucking company? Their passion knew no limits as they raced full speed toward love.

#11 BELOVED INTRUDER
By Noelle Berry McCue
Shannon Douglas hated

Michael Brady from the moment he brought the breezes of life into her shadowy existence. Yet a specter of the past remained to torment her and threaten their future. Could he subdue the demons that haunted her, and carry her to true happiness?

#12 HUNTER'S PAYNE
By Joan J. Domning
P. Lee Payne strode into Karen Hunter's office demanding to know why she was stalking him. She was determined to interview the mysterious photographer. She uncovered his concealed emotions, but could the secrets their hearts confided protect their love, or would harsh daylight shatter their fragile alliance?

#13 TIGER LADY
By Joan J. Domning
Who *was* this mysterious lover she'd never seen who courted her on the office computer, and nicknamed her Tiger Lady? And could he compete with Larry Hart, who came to repair the computer

and stayed to short-circuit her emotions? How could she choose between poetry and passion—between soul and Hart?

#14 STORMY VOWS
By Iris Johansen
Independent Brenna Sloan wasn't strong enough to reach out for the love she needed, and Michael Donovan knew only how to take—until he met Brenna. Only after a misunderstanding nearly destroyed their happiness, did they surrender to their fiery passion.

#15 BRIEF DELIGHT
By Helen Mittermeyer
Darius Chadwick felt his chest tighten with desire as Cygnet Melton glided into his life. But a prelude was all they knew before Cyg fled in despair, certain she had shattered the dream they had made together. Their hearts had collided in an instant; now could they seize the joy of enduring love?

#16 A VERY RELUCTANT KNIGHT
By Billie Green
A tornado brought them together in a storm cel-

lar. But Maggie Sims and Mark Wilding were anything but perfectly matched. Maggie wanted to prove he was wrong about her. She knew they didn't belong together, but when he caressed her, she was swept up in a passion that promised a lifetime of love.

#17 TEMPEST AT SEA
By Iris Johansen
Jane Smith sneaked aboard playboy-director Jake Dominic's yacht on a dare. The muscled arms that captured her were inescapable—and suddenly Jane found herself agreeing to a month-long cruise of the Caribbean. Jane had never given much thought to love, but under Jake's tutelage she discovered its magic . . . and its torment.

#18 AUTUMN FLAMES
By Sara Orwig
Lily Dunbar had ventured too far into the wilderness of Reece Wakefield's vast Chilean ranch; now an oncoming storm thrust her into his arms . . . and he refused to let her go. Could he lure her, step by seductive step, away from the life she had forged for herself, to find her real home in his arms?

#19 PFARR LAKE AFFAIR
By Joan J. Domning
Leslie Pfarr hadn't been back at her father's resort for an hour before she was pitched into the lake by Eric Nordstrom! The brash teenager who'd made her childhood a constant torment had grown into a handsome man. But when he began persuading her to fall in love, Leslie wondered if she was courting disaster.

#20 HEART ON A STRING
By Carla Neggers
One look at heart surgeon Paul Houghton Welling told JoAnna Radcliff he belonged in the stuffy society world she'd escaped for a cottage in Pigeon Cove. She firmly believed she'd never fit into his life, but he set out to show her she was wrong. She was the puppet master, but he knew how to keep her heart on a string.

#21 THE SEDUCTION OF JASON

By Fayrene Preston

On vacation in Martinique, Morgan Saunders found Jason Falco. When a misunderstanding drove him away, she had to win him back. Morgan acted as a seductress, to tempt him to return; she sent him tropical flowers to tantalize him; she wrote her love in letters twenty feet high—on a billboard that echoed the words in her heart.

#22 BREAKFAST IN BED

By Sandra Brown

For all Sloan Fairchild knew, Hollywood had moved to San Francisco when mystery writer Carter Madison stepped into her bed-and-breakfast inn. In his arms the forbidden longing that throbbed between them erupted. Sloan had to choose—between her love for him and her loyalty to a friend. . . .

#23 TAKING SAVANNAH

By Becky Combs

The Mercedes was headed straight for her! Cassie hurled a rock that smashed the antique car's taillight. The price driver Jake Kilrain exacted was a passionate kiss, and he set out to woo the Southern lady, Cassie, but discovered that his efforts to conquer the lady might end in his own surrender . . .

#24 THE RELUCTANT LARK

By Iris Johansen

Her haunting voice had earned Sheena Reardon fame as Ireland's mournful dove. Yet to Rand Challon the young singer was not just a lark but a woman whom he desired with all his heart. Rand knew he could teach her to spread her wings and fly free, but would her flight take her from him or into his arms forever?